THE FRATERNITY

The Fraternity

by

Rosemary Friedman

Dales Large Print Books
Long Preston, North Yorkshire,
BD23 4ND, England.

British Library Cataloguing in Publication Data.

Friedman, Rosemary
      The fraternity.

         A catalogue record of this book is
         available from the British Library

         ISBN   978-1-84262-746-4 pbk

Dales Large Print is an imprint of Library Magna Books Ltd.

Printed and bound in Great Britain by
T.J. (International) Ltd., Cornwall, PL28 8RW

To D.

PART ONE

One

'She had a large cervical polyp,' Amy said. 'These mushroom things are delicious.'

'Have another. They look so sad at breakfast time. What about the biopsy?'

'I haven't had the result yet. I'm not worried. I'll push her haemoglobin up and send her home. How does it feel to have been married for twenty-five years?'

'Quite unbelievable. A quarter of a century!'

'A significant twenty-five years.' Amy twirled the ice in her glass. 'Penicillin … Belsen … Hiroshima … astronauts shooting off in all directions…'

'The nadir and the zenith.'

'You have evidence nearer home.'

'Grant?' Hilda glanced at her son, head and shoulders above the group, which surrounded him in the centre of the room.

'And Peach.'

Peach walked round with the mushroom vol-au-vents on their silver dish and thought Christopher Isherwood only he was a camera and I am a tape-recorder. They're doing research on cocktail party noise; you can listen to someone talking to you with one ear and keep the other roving to pick up relevant information from the far side of the room.

'Where's Mother?' Grant said.

'Still talking to Amy.'

'What about?'

'Cervical polyps.'

'Polypi. She ought to circulate.'

'You tell her.'

'You know the tenth,' Elliot said, describing a curve with his potato crisp, 'where it comes back to the clubhouse; I was on the green for one, it's only a short hole of course, and then believe it or not I messed up a six-foot putt. After that I couldn't do a thing right.'

'This shindig must have been on your mind,' Graham Manning said. 'What do you do with your varicose veins these days?'

'Send them to Sharples. I always have done.'

'I use this new chap Millory. He takes twice as long as Sharples but I think he gets a better result.'

'I'm quite happy with Sharples,' Elliot said. 'Besides, we have a regular game.'

'Your daughter's looking very pretty tonight.'

'Peach? Yes.'

'Still no intention of following in the

family footsteps?'

'Not a hope. She hates it all.'

'Can't blame her in a way. Did you hear that Hodge's boy was short-listed for the death vacancy in Ilford?'

'It's all done with diuretics,' Basil Pratt said. 'Thank you, they look delicious.'

'They're very hot,' Peach said.

'He gives them massive doses and naturally they lose pounds. They put it all back again of course within a month or two.'

'Nice little racket.'

'You're absolutely right. He has a flat in Hyde Park Gate.'

'Bit of a jump from Catford.'

'Goes up to eighty-five in third,' Harry Coningsby said. 'Eighty-five and steady as a rock at a hundred and five.'

'I'm fed up with mine,' Arthur Pritchard said. 'Like driving a tank round the streets.'

'Why don't you flog it?'

'I'd like to. We've just had a new baby.'

'Of course. Congratulations. Who delivered it?'

'Hilda, of course.'

'Everything go off all right?'

'Fine.'

'Good. It's a relief, isn't it? I had a deep transverse arrest in primip. of eighteen last week; insisted on having it at home. Phillips

13

admitted her and had to do a caesarean section.'

'Don't you think he's getting a bit past it?'

'Phillips? Not at all.'

'Mushroom vol-au-vent?' Peach said. 'Be careful. They're hot.'

'"Look", I said, "if that chap's not got a carcinoma of the colon I'll eat my hat."'

'And had he?'

'Well of course he had. That was a year ago. We did an end-to-end anastomosis but he had metastases all over the place.'

'Wasn't he the chap with the dirty bookshop in the Strand? I remember you telling me about him.'

'He was, but I'm afraid he won't be for much longer. Mushroom? No thanks. I don't mind another gin and tonic, dear. Good-looking girl, Elliot's.'

'Where's your daughter these days?'

'Doing Endocrinology at Yale. Haven't seen her for a year.'

'"Like hell," I said, "I'm taking a partner *before* I get my coronary. What with the extra loading and tax-relief it comes to the same thing, anyway. I'm not working myself to death for that ungrateful mob."'

'Thank you, Peach. Don't go away – I'll have another. Not going in for medicine, are you? Sensible girl. Run as fast, and as far as you can, before you get every spark and sparkle of decency and enterprise strangled out of you by the Health Service.'

'"Look," I said, "my husband is a dedicated surgeon. If you must do your duty, find somebody else to give a ticket to..."'

'It was three o'clock before he came home and at five Mulligan's wife went into labour...'

'...affected ass, he always uses gold needles...'

'...no Theatre Sister, so he laid up the trolley himself before you could say knife...'

'...charged her twenty guineas and she went away as happy as a sandboy. I'd told her exactly that for nothing, but of course that wasn't the same thing at all...'

'...you try sewing up a perineum by the light of a twenty-five-watt bulb...'

'...think he needs ECT himself. They're all whacky, if you ask me...'

'...how much did you pull in from the vaccinations?'

'"I'm sorry," he said, "but Sir Harmstrong's just stepped acrorst the street to 'ave a word with Sir Hanthony." "Well, you'd better look slippy," I said, "and step acrorst the street after him, before we have a ruptured aneurysm on our hands..."'

'...eight visits in an hour...'

'...can't work like that, I like to take my time...'

'...did you hear the one about the chappie who went to the woman doctor complaining of...'

'What was it, Mother?' Grant said, taking Hilda's empty glass.
'An ectopic.'
'No. Your drink. You ought to circulate.'
'Of course. Just tell me briefly, Amy. Whisky, Grant, and look after my little Pathologist – she's just arrived.'
'The girl with the red hair? It will be a pleasure.'

She had very white teeth and blushed, the colour clashing with her hair.
'I've been detailed to look after you. I'm Grant Gatehouse.'
'My name is Marshall; Lesley Marshall.'
'Pleased to meet you, Dr Marshall.'

'And you, "Dr" Gatehouse?'

'I don't know. Results of the Finals next week.'

'I wish you luck.'

'Thank you. A drink?'

'Sherry, please.' She had rounded arms, lightly freckled and reminded Grant of summer.

'Dry or medium?'

'Anything. Just to be sociable.'

'You look an unlikely Pathologist.'

'No one looks very likely these days.'

Her dress was sleeveless and he had a sudden desire to kiss the top of her arm. She stood near the door.

'Come and meet someone,' Grant said.

'Do you mind if I just stay here?'

'Not at all. I thought you'd rather...'

'I'm quite happy.'

The eyes were green, black-flecked.

'Look, I have to fill a few glasses. I'll be back.'

'I'll still be here.'

The white teeth.

'Darling, Professor Lindsay wants his coat. He's looking after the Chancellor, you know.'

'What's the mater with him?' Peach said.

Professor Lindsay's eyebrows shot up into his egghead.

'A "stomach complaint" according to the newspapers. They don't give me a moment's

17

peace with their wretched little notebooks.'

'It will all be worth it in the next Birthday Honours. If you want any help, Ian, you know where to find me.'

'I'll put in a word for you, Elliot, but I think Miss Dullally whom I have in the next room to the Chancellor might interest you more.'

'The one with the bosom? I saw her in that film where she fell in the water every five minutes.'

'Remarkable breasts,' Professor Lindsay said. 'Truly remarkable!'

'A grey,' Professor Lindsay said at the bottom of the stairs. He straightened his bow tie, then examined his impeccable nails. 'My demi-saison. You know, Peach, you have exceptional parents. Quite exceptional.'

'I know.'

'How do you?'

'Everyone says so.'

'I'd like you to meet my son. He does Orthopaedic Surgery at the South-West London. Good-looking, too. Takes after his mother.'

'That would be nice,' Peach said. 'I'll get your coat.'

'He wants me to meet his son,' Peach said. 'He's at the South-West London.'

'Hopkins' Senior Registrar,' Grant said.

'MS at twenty-five. Not bad going. Didn't you tell him you don't mix with the fraternity?'

'I didn't want to be rude. He'll forget all about it, anyway.'

'He didn't get to be Professor of Medicine because of his bad memory.'

'I'll deal with it when the time comes. Don't let me keep you from that red-head.'

'Extraordinary perception.'

'Not at all. You look in her direction at least once every five seconds. I thought you'd developed a tic for a moment.'

'It's been wonderful, Hilda. Best of luck for the next twenty-five.'

'Thank you. And thank you for coming.'

'Where's Elliot?'

'Somewhere around. Won't you have one more drink?'

'Thank you, no. I still have a couple of visits to do on the way back.'

'Today?'

'I'm on rota duty. I shouldn't really be here. I'm sending a gynae. case to your Out-patients. A Mrs Penrose, query metropathia.'

'I'll look out for her,' Hilda said. 'There's Elliot now?'

She'd finished her sherry.

'Let me get you another,' Grant said.

'No, really.'

He took her glass.

'I have to go.'

'You've only just arrived. I would have come back before. Had to be sociable.'

'I'll say goodbye to your mother.'

'Let me run you home.'

'I have my car outside.'

'A little longer. Things are just starting to hum.'

'Really not. I have enjoyed it.'

'As you wish.'

'I wish.'

'Look Lesley…'

She was easing her way across the room.

'If you tie it off just there,' Mr Swallow said, pushing aside a dish of olives and drawing a quick neat diagram on the white tablecloth, 'you'll get very little bleeding into the cavity. I've been doing it for years.'

'…gives a beautiful anaesthetic, lowers the blood pressure right down…'

'…great obese chap, be dead in a year. "Want to make a quick thou., Doc?" he says. "Singmo Rubber, and keep it under your hat."'

'What happened?'

'This was two years ago. But there's a very nice little Property Company coming up: a pale of mine's a director…'

20

'...busybody on the Management Committee says there's a simple answer to that. Your Children's Ward is practically empty, take some of them for Men's Surgical for the time being. "My dear lady," I said, "you try fitting a six-foot coal-heaver with a fractured femur into a four-foot cot..."'

'Have you lost her?' Peach said.
  'She went home.'
  'Poor Grant. Deadly, isn't it?'
  'The party? I'm rather enjoying it.'
  'Do you think I've stayed long enough? There's a do at Sarah's.'
  'You'd better square it with Mother.'
  'I was just going to slip out.'

'How do you think it's going, Hilda?'
  'Fine. What are they all looking at?'
  'Grant. He's doing his imitation of Mao-Tse Tung. Where's Amy off to?'
  'I have an Egyptian girl in labour. She's going to take a peep at her for me.'

'Elliot dear, it's been delightful.'
  'Amy; I hear you're of to do my wife's work.'
  'I have a strong suspicion she'd rather go herself.'

'Mother, do you mind if I leave? Sarah's party – remember?'

'Of course, dear. Peach, this is Dr Sims. He practises in Sevenoaks and has three delightful girls.'

'Boys,' Dr Sims said. 'Which branch of the healing art are you going to embrace?'

'None,' Peach said.

'Ha! A renegade.'

'Where are you going?' Elliot said.

'Sarah's.'

'Thought there was someone missing.'

'She has a do of her own.'

'I expect someone can give you a lift.' He looked round vaguely.

'Don't worry, I'll get the bus.'

'Ah, Elliot, tracked you down!'

'Pettigrew! Good to see you.'

'I'm off,' Peach said.

'Who was that?'

'My daughter.'

Two

The bus was brightly lit, the conductor black. Legs apart, braced against the jolting, he logged his journey, blue uniform crumpled. Peach, sitting sideways, watched him. South Ken. at night, dark falling, a far cry from Trinidad, hot sun, pineapples, singing, dancing: a deception, of course; probably lived in a shack with umpteen others, not very much to eat either, otherwise why had he come to put up with the endless humiliations, the tight-lipped shop assistants, uncompromising landladies, self-righteous within their white skins. In America it was worse of course, he'd have to walk miles perhaps to use a lavatory, buy a meal. What must it be like to be at the receiving end of a hatred, a disgust?

The bus jolted to a halt. No one got on or off. He put up a brown hand, fingers pale-tipped, and pressed the bell.

Xenophobia; there's something about the blacks; the smell; you can't stay in the same room. I don't know what it is; something. I don't like tomatoes. Don't pretend there's anything intrinsically wrong with tomatoes. The dislike is in your mind, a self-

23

chosen attitude.

What must you think of us?

He put away the board on which he was writing. Slid it into a slot under the stairs, curled an arm round the chrome rail on the platform, began to whistle. Perhaps it wasn't so bad; he had a job, three meals, roof over his head. Bread alone. You had to be able to lift your head as well. What are you thinking? That I'm thinking about you? Anything? End of the run? Tea, scalding hot? Wife and kids? Home? You know, Peach, you have exceptional parents. I know. How do you? Everyone says so. Everyone. Elliot with his doting patients vomiting and bleeding at mealtimes. Hilda's mother's rupturing membranes, dilating, at extraordinary moments, with urgency. Grant, caught up in the maelstrom, Dr Sims dreary from Sevenoaks.

He stopped whistling and called the name of Sarah's road in clipped accents. Peach stood beside him on the platform. You and I both; outside is a lonely place; stepped down onto the pavement, into the lamplit road.

The door of Sarah's flat was opened by a hollow stomached boy in black jeans she hadn't seen before.

'Hallo darling,' he said.

'Where's Sarah?'

'Around.' He walked away and was swallowed up by the music from the sitting-room.'

24

The curtains in Sarah's bedroom weren't drawn and shadowed legs visible almost to the knee teetered on pale heels or strode creepily singly or in pairs along the Cromwell Road. Only the lamp was lit with the rose-spattered shade that Sarah had made so that you couldn't see the damp patches on the wallpaper and barely your face in the spotted mirror.

Sarah came from Wales and had long faded blonde hair, which clung to her face, moved softly, dreamily. Her father was a judge and she absorbed the laws of Contract and the intricacies of the Constitution with the same facility and lack of effort with which she attracted men. They gravitated automatically towards her, allured, Peach often thought, by her complete repose, a magnetic stillness from the centre of which she smoked her eternal cigarette, exhaling the smoke with a downward movement of her eyes which sent her part-blonde lashes splaying against her cheek.

In the mirror Peach saw Ronnie come in. He put an arm round her neck and rummaged in a dressing-table drawer in which there were non-ironed handkerchiefs, an open pancake make-up, some amber beads, hair rollers, a packet of Kleenex, and some bent photographs.

'What are you looking for?'

'Socks.' He extricated one black one and

looked unsuccessfully for its mate.

Peach had once been surprised at Sarah's promiscuity. In their first week at college there had been a bearded giant from the Art Faculty, and after a while a third year Law student, then a couple of medics and an earnest biochemist who stuttered and many more whom Peach couldn't remember, and currently, Ronnie. They came as if they were merely additions to her wardrobe and were released with no more animosity than her cast-off clothes. Her blatant sexuality was a need, which Sarah indulged with as little emotion as she cut bread and butter.

Ronnie found his other sock and was gone. Peach gave up trying to see her face in the dim light and went towards the music. She stopped in the doorway looking for Sarah.

The boy in black jeans ladled punch into a used glass and handed it to her. He felt her cheekbones with light fingertips and standing back, looked at her through half-closed eyes.

'Interesting,' he said, 'veeery interesting.'

'Where's Sarah?'

He nodded towards the divan.

Peach eased her way through oblivious dancers gyrating on the floor. Sarah detached herself from the arms and legs on the divan.

'Hallo, darling.' She kissed Peach. 'You managed to get away. What did I miss?'

'Dr Sims from Sevenoaks,' Peach said. 'Mother demonstrating a breech with a cheese straw, venesections over the vol-au-vents...'

'Relax, honey-chile,' Sarah said. 'You're with Momma now.'

A young man in a suit sat in the hearth and watched them.

'I must do something about the punch,' Sarah said. 'It's getting dreggy.'

'Come and sit down, Melba,' Irving said from the divan.

It was solid with bodies, hair, jerseys.

'Where do you suggest?'

'Dress circle,' Irving indicated his lap. She sat down in the hearth next to the young man in the suit.

'I'm cut to the quick,' Irving said.

He had square wrists, was thin, all angles.

'You don't think much of the medical profession?' He raised one blond eyebrow.

'In its place. Not to live with.'

'She was only a doctor's daughter,' Irving said.

'Shut up.'

'It's quite clean.'

'Irving,' Fleur said, 'are my ribs by any chance hurting your elbow?'

'I'm Henry,' he said. 'Melba?'

'Peach.'

'Someone has great imagination.'

'On the contrary. When I was born,

Mother's friend, who delivered her, said: "It's a girl, Hilda, and an absolute peach." Mother said: "Peach! What a wonderful name – don't you think so, Amy?" And that was that. I've always hated it.'

She wondered what he was doing there. Henry.

'Sarah's never mentioned you.'

'I came with Fleur.'

'You don't look like a friend of Fleur's.'

'You don't look like a friend of Sarah's.'

She looked down at the black dress she had put on for the Silver Wedding party, conspicuous among the tight pants and flats.

'We're at college together.'

Ronnie turned off the record player. 'Look, shut up a moment everybody.'

The dancers stayed entwined.

'Floor!'

'Chair!'

'Speech!'

'For-hor he's a jolly good fellow…'

'Christabel angel, take your hair out of my mouth…'

'I want to know who's marching on Monday,' Ronnie said. 'There are a few last-minute arrangements to be made and we need some volunteers for the banners.'

There was an enthusiastic show of waving arms and legs. Only Peach and Henry sat still.

'What's up with you two?' Ronnie said.

'I don't like crowds, Ronnie,' Peach said. 'Mass anything.'

'What about you?' Eyes were focused on Henry.

'You can march till your feet drop off,' Henry said. 'It won't make the slightest difference.'

'Not if you sit on your complacent arse it won't,' Ronnie said.

'March from here to Land's End,' Henry said without raising his voice, 'to Timbuctoo, if you like. The Bomb is here.'

'It's here, let's face,' Irvin said, 'but at least we can make an effort to repair the damage before it's too late.'

'We've had centuries to make amends,' Henry said. 'Now we've done the damage, all of us have, and if the bomb was banned tomorrow one of our charming, civilised fellow human beings would invent something even more revolting by Tuesday morning.'

'What are we going to do about it then, Daddy-O?' A voice from the floor by the record player said.

'It's hard to say,' Henry said. 'I think *people* will have to change... To stop being so malicious, distrustful...'

'You want a bloody lot, cock!'

'Not us,' Henry said, calmly. 'You and I can hear the reaper.'

'And where will you be with your pi-jaw Daddy-O when they drop a nice big fat

29

juicy one on London.'

'Oddly enough,' Henry said, 'I can bear the thought of total destruction. It's the everyday individual cruelties that nauseate me; pick up any newspaper...'

'Wrap up!'

'I'm not against marching...' Henry said.

'Give him a medal, somebody!'

'...only its limitations.'

They started shouting all at once. A girl in a fringed jumper hurled a cushion at Ronnie. Peach picked her way out to the tiny cupboard that was Sarah's kitchen.

'Who's murdering who?' Sarah said, cutting bananas into the punch bowl.

'Henry dropped a clanger. He's against the march. Who is he?'

Sarah looked at her, then went back to the banana. 'I don't really know. Some odd relation of Fleur's, I believe.' The bananas were finished. She stood back to see the effect, then looked vaguely round the kitchen.

'I suppose you can't put prunes in punch?'

'Absolutely not.'

'It looks terribly unpopulated.'

Ronnie came in with a handkerchief held to his eye and his hair on end.

'What happened, Sweetie?'

'I walked into a fist.' He ran the cold tap. Sarah took the handkerchief from him.

'Come to Momma,' she said.

The sitting-room floor was a tangling mass

of male bodies. The girls stood on the divan and the three chairs, cheering them on.

Peach went into Sarah's room and sat down on the bed to wait until it was all over.

Three

He came in rubbing his knuckles. He was very tall, slightly older than Sarah's crowd.

'You've hurt your hand.'

'Someone ran into it.'

'Is it bleeding?'

He put it in his pocket. 'It's nothing. I wondered where you'd got to.'

'I was just waiting until they calmed down. Ronnie gets very excited.'

'And you hate crowds.' He sat on the bed next to her.

'I have visions of being crushed.' There'd been a carnival when she was a child, grotesque animal heads twenty feet high, a surging mass of bodies, streamers, hysterical laughter... She'd screamed to be taken home. 'Carnivals as a child.' She shuddered.

'The headless lady my personal fascination; at the funfair. I spent every penny I had.'

'She looks so real.'

'She *is* real.' He wasn't smiling. 'Amazing the way they keep her alive; all those tubes, bottles of blood and things.'

'The five-inch lady in the goldfish bowl.'

'That's a hoax, of course. All done with mirrors.'

'The headless lady…?' He couldn't be serious.

'I still go whenever I get the chance. I give her commands. Wave! And she waves. Scratch your nose! That foxes her. You'd ban the bomb, though?'

'I don't know. I face in all directions.'

'That's pretty awkward for a lawyer.'

'Who told you…?'

'You said you were at College with Sarah.'

He forgot nothing.

'The Arts Faculty was full.'

The Dean of the Law Faculty had no illusions. 'Why do you wish to read Law, Miss Gatehouse?' Because I don't want to do Medicine and there is no room in the Arts Faculty for another year and my father thinks I should be at university and there is nothing else I particularly want to do. 'I would like to become a barrister.' He believed it no more than she did. He was a grey man, weary, with a job to do. 'You'll give it up to get married,' he said, making notes. 'They all do.'

'And you're a doctor's daughter,' Henry said.

'Twice over. Obstetrician and Gynae-cologist for a mother and GP for a father.

33

Brother Grant has just taken his Finals, results next Thursday; but Gatehouses never fail. Not the medical ones, anyway.'

'You really hate it?'

'You try living in a cross between the departure platform at Victoria Station and a receiving room.'

'In a good cause, surely?'

'They think so.'

'And you...?'

'I don't love people. Mankind as a sort of sterile mass but not individuals with their horrid complaints. I can't put out my hand. I never have been able to. They think I'm odd. I come to Sarah's.'

He rubbed his knuckles. 'Pretty odd bunch here.'

'They get a bit worked up over the bomb; Ronnie does, but at least you know when you've finished talking they'll still be there. You don't find yourself addressing the wall.'

She couldn't see in the dim light whether the stripes on his tie were blue or green. It worried her.

The record player started up in the other room.

'...*you can bring Pearl she's a darn nice girl*...'

'Everybody dance!' Ronnie's voice.

'...*but don't bring Lulu.*'

'The differences appear to be settled,'

Henry said.

'You put the cat among the pigeons.'

'...*you can bring Rose with the turned-up nose*...'

'When I was Ronnie's age I felt the same way.'

'You're not that much older.'

He buttoned his jacket. 'It's the little difference that makes the big difference.'

'...*she's the kind of smartie, breaks up every party*...'

'I have to go.'

She waited among the duffels to give her telephone number, say when she was free.

'This is the first time I've met a Peach.'

'...*Lulu gets blue when she goes cuckoo*...'

'I'll just find Sarah; thank her.'

She went with him into the blare of the sitting-room. He ducked his head automatically in the doorway.

'...*When she gets the feeling ... the boys all hit the ceiling*...'

He looked over their heads for Sarah.

Irving grabbed her. 'Dance, darling.' He spun her off her feet.

'...*Hulabalulu don't bring Lulu, she'll come by herseeeeeelf!*'

When she looked round Henry was gone.

'Seven forty-five,' Grant said.

She was surprised to find that it was morning; remembered Henry. Perhaps he would phone.

'Monday morning!' Grant opened the curtains.

She pulled the sheet up to her chin.

'I haven't done my essay for the Tutorial.'

'There's a letter.' He spun it onto the bed.

She put out a hand for the envelope with its Canadian stamp. 'From Parker.'

'When's he coming back?'

'Friday.'

'How was it at Sarah's?'

She thought of Henry. 'Fine. I'm expecting a phone call.'

'What's his name?'

'Henry. Tell him... Tell him I'll be back at five.'

'I'll run your bath,' Grant said, 'since I've nothing better to do, till Thursday.'

'Slowly!'

She turned over and spread the pages on the pillow.

'Baby,' Parker's letter began.

'Sponge him down with tepid water and I'll see him after Surgery,' Elliot said into the telephone.

Peach removed a packet from the Harley Biological Laboratories from her plate and sat down. 'What's in here?' There was a covered silver entrée dish.

'Wilted sandwiches from last night,' Grant said. 'Sardine. Can you think of "a suitable binding for damaged bone" in six letters?'

Hilda looked over the top of her glasses. 'Riband.'

Elliot answered the phone, then held his hand over the receiver. 'For you, Miss Hallam; about the pre-med for your hysterectomy,' he said.

Hilda took the glasses off. 'I've already told Sister.'

Elliot passed her the receiver and Peach ate toast with the cord an inch away from her nose.

'Hundred and fiftieth of atropine and a third of omnopon. Why she had to bother me I don't know.' Hilda passed the receiver back.

'What about a "college window" in five letters?'

'When you've finished mutilating the newspaper,' Peach said. 'You've all day with nothing to do and I'm late.'

'I'll give you a lift if you like,' Hilda said. 'I start my list at nine-thirty.'

Elliot poured coffee with one hand and dialled with the other.

'EBS? I have a man of sixty-five with acute retention…'

Peach wondered if Henry would phone.

Elliot stood up, brushing the crumbs from his suit.

'I left a bottle of Staph. Toxoid. Somewhere.'

Peach pointed. 'Next to the jam. No – the

other side.'

'If the EBS rings back, take a message, Grant.'

'We have to leave in ten minutes,' Hilda said.

They sat stationary in the traffic against the beige leather upholstery like Royalty. What did one talk about to one's mother when she inhabited a world a hundred miles away?

'Busy morning?'

'Routine,' Hilda said. 'Couple of fibroids, hysterectomy, Bartholin's cyst. What about you?'

The traffic ahead began to move, slowly. She watched Mann's leather gloves deal expertly with the gears.

'Constitutional Law. Contracts and a tutorial. It was a good party.'

'You're always together.'

'Socially, I mean.'

She didn't pursue the matter. Wherever they were they were constantly chewing over the same old cases.

'I have a locum anaesthetist.'

'What happened to Maurice?'

'He's touring the Greek Islands. His name's Cronshaw. He's terribly slow. I'm used to Maurice.'

They stopped again, this time for traffic lights.

'The traffic gets worse and worse.' Hilda

drummed her fingers on the arm-rest and peered out of the window as if it would help.

'Couldn't we cut down Fitzroy Street?'

'No right turn,' Mann said into the mirror.

'Do you think Grant has passed his exams?' Hilda said.

'No doubt. Chip of the old block.'

'Better than having one on your shoulder,' Hilda said mildly. 'Good – we're moving.'

'I suppose you mean me?'

'You are a bit prickly.'

'I'm just hopelessly outnumbered.'

'I can't understand why you don't just relax...'

God. Screaming God.

'...take no notice.'

'A bit difficult. Omnopon with breakfast.'

'Surely after eighteen years...'

There was no point in arguing. Hilda was crossing off things in her diary with a silver pencil. She had square nails, very short. Peach thought of Sarah's, frosted white, long like a tiger's.

They turned into Gower Street.

'I hope you aren't too late.' There was relief in Hilda's voice as Mann drew up smoothly at the kerb.

He got out and opened the door for her.

'See you tonight,' Hilda said.

Don't take any wooden nickels. Parker always said that. Tiptoe through the fibroids. 'Bye.' Peach waggled two fingers, watching them drive off down Gower Street.

'...The issue of an Order in Council under the Foreign Jurisdiction Acts is a Legislative act...'

She shut the door of the Eugenics theatre quietly and crept down the steps to the row where Sarah was sitting.

Professor Ramsay glared at her. 'North Charterland Exploration Company v. The King...'

'What happened to you?' Sarah hissed.

'Got up late. Long letter from Parker. Traffic.'

'He's in a filthy temper.'

'If the young ladies would be so kind as to pay attention,' Professor Ramsay said in a thin voice.

Peach attempted a contrite look and opening her notebook, wrote 'Henry' in the margin. She didn't even know his other name.

Four

On Thursday morning Grant was surprised to find that on the day which had seemed so impossibly remote through six years of Biology, Anatomy, Physiology, Medicine and Surgery, the thought uppermost in his mind was a girl with red hair and freckled arms.

'Dr Gatehouse,' he said into the mirror, in the bathroom. It had a familiar sound.

'Dr *Grant* Gatehouse.' Better.

He'd never seen such white teeth; good figure, too, everything in the right place.

He shaved carefully as if it was going to make a difference, shaking the kaleidoscope of reflections.

Days, weeks, months, years, spent with Gray's *Anatomy*. Had he really committed the two thousand pages to memory? The brain now, that was a complex structure, interesting too; perhaps Neurosurgery, long hours on the feet; fascinating though the brain.

The dissecting-room, nervous ribaldry, nausea; later on easy familiarity with the arm, the leg, the pelvis that occupied one's waking moments until its structure was seared, etched indelibly upon the mind. First days on the wards all thumbs and blushes and dropping stethoscopes knowing they were laughing at you, the nurses and the patients, because you were neither flesh nor fowl. How did one talk to a patient, command respect from a nurse twice as old and twenty times as experienced? It came and it passed pleasantly enough. Good times, rags, poker in the Common Room, notice on the door 'coitus don't interruptus'; taking blood from each other's veins, vaccinating each other, swallowing stomach tubes, declaring passionate, undying love to pretty nurses, feeling asinine when Quail or Macdonald wiped the floor with you. 'What did you say your diagnosis was, Mr Gatehouse?' And you hadn't been listening, thinking of last night or the night to come or going to Italy in the Long Vac., anything but the patient in the bed. Buggering up the anatomy because of Laila for love of whom you nearly chucked everything until she took off for Paris and a night-club talent spotter in a camel-hair coat. In and out of the pawnshop with a microscope. Setting up in business with Mitchell as society photographers to finance an overland trip to India; tea with debs.' Mums, man to man talks with debs.' Dads, quick whip round for dinner jackets on the night, disaster as outstanding shots were taken enthusiastically with unloaded cameras. Drinking beer, and Jacques Tati; swotting all night, knowing it was impossible even with Benzedrine and dawn already grey at the window. An entire new field of treatment to be mastered, chemotherapy, steroids. First day on the district alone; who was the elephantine mound in the bed screaming for? Ow, me! Run a mile; you've had it mate, stop shaking, take that sickly grin off, up with your sleeves and deliver that baby. I did it! Eureka! Alone I did it. 'Not a thing to worry about, Mrs Smith. You just go to sleep!' Pleased as Punch. Hop on the bicycle, look, no hands, like a ten-year-old, whoops! That was a near one. Pull yourself together, you're tired. Another human being in the world and I did it! They came in and went out. The first encounter with death. The sheepish removal of the stethoscope from a heart no longer beating; inevitable theological arguments. Beer to drown doubt; obscenity the thin veneer of horror. Mangled bodies and suicides in Casualty, gently down the slipway in Geriatrics, confusion in Medical and Surgical, oddly enough none protesting. Smells; ether, phenol, cabbage, no longer smelled. Derision of Chiefs respected; love's lows and highs; aching fingers; personal shorthand; coffee in retorts; foetuses in bottles; clean, shiny diagrams and bloody reality. The child, the old man, the paralytic, giving birth to thoughts of a career in accountancy or the Civil Service. Christmas ward-shows growing more and more incomprehensible with the sinking level of beer in the barrel; neat incisions in the turkey; drunken fumblings in the sluice. Whiffs of ether; milligrams of pethidine; seeking, searching in fun or earnest. Jazz, poker dice, skeleton in the bedroom, feverish parties with French-letter balloons; religion, politics, blind, desperate allegiances to people, causes. Fun, work...

Suddenly it was over.

Or was it? He washed his razor under the tap and was aware of a hollow, unfamiliar sensation in his lower abdomen. Perhaps he was ill: that would be a laugh. He went into his room and lying on the bed palpated his abdomen.

'I came to wish you luck,' Elliot said, coming in. 'What's the matter?'

'I'm not sure. Some guarding on the right side...'

Elliot put a hand on his abdomen. 'Nonsense. Butterflies.'

'You sure?'

'Call in a Consultant if you like!'

They had grey faces, smoked nervously, had given one to the alabaster bust of Queen Victoria that dominated the dank hall. The clock jumped slow minutes; there was little talking, much pacing; black mingled with

44

white, not-so-young with young; fourth-time Hurstmonceaux in Savile Row suit. The glass doors were opened. Nervous, like gazelles, they crowded round.

A tedium of unfamiliar numbers. Victims for selection they presented themselves one by one at the doors.

'...number eight, number ten, number twenty-two, number fifteen.' A desperate Bingo session. 'Number ninety-four...'

'That's you, you clot!' Berry said.

Grant walked on rubber legs through the doors and up to the desk.

'Number ninety-four?' The Clerk peered at Grant, his list.

'Yes.' Get on with it.'

'Mr Gatehouse?'

'Yes.'

'Pleased to say you have passed. Congratulations.'

As simple as that.

He made way for number twenty-three who looked as if he was about to be sick.

In the sunlit square they mingled with the red and yellow tulips. Clive had passed and so had Berry; the two women, Sheila and Patsy, Johnson from Singapore, Webb from Bechuanaland, Big Jim from Jamaica, all except Hollis who desperately needed to for financial reasons.

'Hurstmonceaux?'

'Pipped again.'

'Fourth time, isn't it?'

They watched him drive off in his Alfa Romeo.

'I *feel* exactly the same,' Grant said. 'Do I look any different.'

'Like a Cheshire cat,' Berry said. 'What do we do now?'

'Spread the word.'

There was a hundred-yard queue outside the telephone box.

'No joy there.'

'Think I'll pop round to the Hospital,' Grand said. 'Just catch my Mama as she's finishing. See you low-lifes tonight.'

'Very well, Doctor,' Berry said. 'And I should take that grin off, or they'll admit you.'

'To Queen Adelaide's?' Grant said.

Queen Adelaide's Hospital for Women looked like a workhouse outside and a public lavatory inside. Next door a concrete tower of glass and curtain-walling emphasised its shame.

'Any idea where I'll find Miss Hallam?'

The porter found his glasses, then his ledger, then his page.

'Miss 'Allam's hoperatin'.'

He shared the lift with a nurse with a kidney dish and a physiotherapist with an outsize bosom.

46

In the changing-room outside the theatre he recognised his mother's coat hung neatly on a hanger and gave a message to a nurse with baby-blue eyes.

Hilda came, green-robed, pulling off hat and rubber gloves.

'Oh, it's you, Grant.' She threw them in the bin. 'I thought it was Elliot. The silly girl said *Doctor* Gatehouse.'

'It is,' Grant said.

Hilda looked puzzled, then remembered.

'Grant!' she said. 'You've passed.'

He kissed her, unable to remember the last time he had done so. She smelled of halothane.

'Have you finished?' he said. He had vague ideas of taking her out to lunch, although she would have to pay.

'I have my mothers to look at yet.'

'OK. Just thought you'd like to know.'

'Dr Cronshaw would like a word with you, Miss Hallam, before we take the patient back to the ward,' the blue-eyed nurse said.

'I'm terribly pleased, Grant.'

He winked at her with affection. 'So am I.'

He ran down the stairs, excited like a child. Fifth floor Maternity, Fourth floor Men's Surgical, Third Floor Paediatrics, X-Ray and Pathology. He stopped, staring at the letters black on white. Pathology. He followed the pointing arrow.

Technicians, perched on stools, bent over

microscopes and slides.

'Dr Marshall?'

A young man with hair flopping over his forehead jerked his head towards a door.

She sat at her desk writing, the freckled arms covered by her white coat.

'Hallo Lesley.' He felt stupid now, having come, disturbed her. 'I've passed my Finals, thought I'd nip in, I was upstairs...'

She put down her pen.

'I'm terribly pleased.'

The white teeth. She really did look pleased.

'How does it feel?'

'No different. Relief perhaps, to have all the exams behind one. They're a bit of a sweat.' He looked out of the window down into the area. He could see the red blankets of the ward in opposite windows, flowers badly arranged in vases that were too small, green screens.

'Walter Mittyish in a way. I see myself as a great surgeon "Sir Grant Gatehouse"; Physician to Royalty; Endocrinologist of international repute. I need cutting down to size.'

She laughed. 'You will be when you get your first house job.'

He leaned both hands on the desk and faced her. 'Come out to lunch, Lesley. Celebrate.'

She flicked through a pile of papers. 'I

48

have all these to go through and the report to make out by three. It's one of those days.'

Grant took the loose change out of his pocket and counted it.

'Just as well.'

'Want to borrow some?'

He wanted to kiss her.

'No thanks. How did you celebrate?'

'When I qualified?'

'Yes.'

He thought she wasn't going to answer for a moment.

'I went home to put my feet up. I was six months pregnant at the time.'

He put the money back carefully in his pocket, piece by piece as if it was liable to break.

'My husband died. I have a child of five.' She looked at her watch. He was being dismissed.

'I'm sorry. I didn't know. Look, Lesley. Can you ever come out?'

She shook her head. 'It's too involved. That's why I told you.' She indicated her work, her face still guarded. 'I really have to get on. I promised Dr Bader. I'm truly pleased about your Finals.'

He went to the door. 'I'll ring you.'

'Please don't.'

'Why?'

'I have … commitments.'

'And I have determination.'

49

'Sometimes,' she said, 'that's an awfully stupid reason for doing things.'

'Time Gentlemen please!' the landlord of *The Crooked Farrow* said.

Grant was aware of a weight on his lap and the smell of sweat and smoke in his nostrils. His eyelids felt like garage doors but he managed to raise them sufficiently to see that the load he carried was a big blonde girl; girl, well she must be pushing forty with half an inch of dark roots and blackheads on the side of her nose. He looked round the room at glasses raised then set onto wet tables, customers drifting to the door calling good night to the melancholy looking cove in the white apron swabbing the bar. He looked for Clive and Berry but couldn't see them, must have lost them somewhere. He forced his mind painfully back. They'd started off at home. Elliot had opened champagne, the foam spilling over onto the table, wetting a pile of pale blue journals. Clive and Berry had been there then, Peach, Hilda, raising their glasses. They'd been very jolly everybody had been jolly something to do with a girl with red hair my husband died he couldn't remember her name, but they'd finished the champagne and gone off in Berry's father's car to a place in Hammersmith Berry knew and worked their way into town. *The Mason's Arms* he remembered and *The*

Wooden Whistle. I had a wooden whistle, Berry said, and it wooden whistle, so I bought a steel whistle, and it steel wooden whistle, so I bought a lead whistle, and they wouldn't lead me whistle, so I bought a tin whistle, and now I tin whistle. They had collapsed at that one leaning against each other the tears pouring down their faces. After that there was a place off Baker Street and *Tiny Tim's* in Soho, Berry and Clive had been there then, he remembered because there'd been some sort of an argument with a fellow in a yellow waistcoat whom Berry had punched in the nose; only the fellow ducked and Berry fell flat on his face. They'd been there too in the place with the piano, downstairs somewhere, because he remembered having to prise Clive away from the piano, over which he had been draped. After that he couldn't remember; certainly not how he came to have ten stone of no lady planted firmly on his lap...

'We gotta go.'

She was saying something, stood up, and it was a great weight off his mind. His mind! Ha, that was a good one, must remember that...

'Come on it's closin' time.'

'If you please, Sir.'

That was a miserable looking cove behind the bar he was coming round, looked nasty...

51

'It's not my fault! 'e won't come.'

'I don't want no trouble now.'

Grant got to his feet synchronising his movements carefully. He pulled himself to his full height, then tottered, the big girl supporting him beneath his arms.

'I,' he said to the miserable looking fellow, 'am Dr Gatehouse!' Of course that was why they were celebrating, Finals day. He'd passed. So had Clive and Berry where the hell were they?

The fellow picked up five glasses in one hand.

'I don't care if you're Dr Kildare. Out!'

'Not very polite, is he?' Grant said to the big girl.

'Come along do,' she said, pulling him towards the door.

'I've half a mind...' he said with dignity.

''Bout all you 'ave got,' the man said, shoving him through the door and locking it after him.

'I'll take you to my place,' the big girl said.

Grant slid down onto the pavement and leaned his head against the wall.

'Call me at six,' he said, 'I have to do an adrenalectomy on the Archbishop.'

She prodded him with the toe of her shoe.

'Fat lot of use you are.'

Five

He hadn't phoned. He could have got her number from Fleur, Sarah, the book, directory... She was obsessed; not just his face, all of him, relaxed in the hearth at Sarah's, his voice, cynical or was it?...'the headless lady my personal fascination ... she *is* real' no trace of a smile. What had she anyway, a few moments at Sarah's, his interest had been fragmentary, polite, and yet and yet. One could usually rely on one's Geiger counter not radiation of course but love, a disease and you had no idea where it began; once it got hold of you though and infiltrated, secondary deposits everywhere, there was no cure, no prophylaxis either because you didn't know when and where it was going to hit you. She had gone to Sarah's just gone, felt him watching as she spoke to Sarah, had to sit beside him, not on Irving's lap, had to. It had happened before. Michael, smooth, with his smooth white Jag, and all the right clothes for all the right occasions everything right except that he had turned out to be an absolutely crashing bore. Patrick from Ireland who in an excess of high spirits and gin had driven them into a tree. Paul who kissed beautifully and threatened suicide if ever she grew tired of him, which she did. Barney with his passion for fresh air; Stanislaus who went to great lengths to avoid it; the thing had clicked for a while at any rate, but you knew, you usually knew right from the word go. No one was immune, bishops athletes actresses and any place, Lyons' Corner House the bus and Covent Garden box-office as well as the more likely places and with your hair anyhow and not prepared, in less than the bat of an eye, and you were floored finished concentration gone dreamless sleep equilibrium you had no choice. She could say to Fleur that fellow you brought to Sarah's ... but what was the point flogging a dead horse? He had been meeting someone yes that was probably it he was already involved no use torturing oneself it was torture too the image was everywhere six foot plus of it closed eyes open walking talking sleeping like the DT's. Five days! Long enough for anyone. She got ready to meet Parker.

'Good to see you Baby,' Parker said.

They were lying on the grass in the park, Parker on his back, arms beneath his head. Peach on her stomach watching the ants weaving in and out amongst the grass stems.

'I missed you,' Parker said.

She wondered if that was what human

beings looked like to God, scurrying, if he suddenly decided to put his thumb on one, half a dozen, six million.

'I missed you too.'

Like the use of a hand. Father Confessor, Sarah said, the antithesis of home. They'd met at College where Parker was reading International Law. Parker was fun.

'Something's happened.' He wore a black leather jacket, white T-shirt.

'No.'

'Yes. What's his name?'

'Henry.'

'I should never have gone away.'

'He doesn't know I exist.'

'Henry who?'

'I don't know. I met him at Sarah's on Sunday.'

'Poor Baby.' He leaned over and kissed her. 'I'll take you dancing.'

There was a students' cellar with a Negro band. She liked dancing with Parker.

'The Sav-oy.'

Peach looked up. 'What happened?'

'I'm loaded, Baby. Filthy, stinking rich. They finally wound up the estate.'

'You never told me about your father.'

'You don't toss someone you love into the conversation like a ball.'

'I didn't know.' She knew nothing about Parker. Imagined him rootless.

'It was a pretty one-sided affair. Pop didn't

love anyone. Only a scrap of green paper. He was in the grocery business. Had a coronary thrombosis in one of his stores. They found him between the canned fruit and the pan-shine. At the funeral there were no friends, only business associates. All Pop cared for was his cut price goods and they didn't send a wreath.

'He wanted me to go in with him of course. When I told him I wanted to do International Law and to work for peace between nations you know what he did Baby? He laughed like a drain. There wasn't going to be no peace, he said, only bigger and better wars. He'd been through the war, Jap prisoner, Burma Road, weighed 84 pounds on liberation. I guess it affected his mind. Ma was in the business too. After he died she sold out. No inspiration any more. She still walks by the stores. "Door mats a dollar ninety" she says, "crazy, and right next to the strawberry jelly". When I'm through College I'll take her on a world cruise.'

'The war did dreadful things to people.'

'Pop had snapshots; what the Japs did. They make you want to throw up.'

'Do you think there'll be another?'

'War? Who knows? We were kids.'

'It seeps out of the last generation, a kind of slime so that even if you don't remember you can't help getting the smell of it, the fear. You think the bomb should be banned?'

'Sure, sure. Ban the bomb and tomorrow there'll be a bigger better one.'

'That's what Henry says.'

'What kind of a guy is he?'

'I told you. I don't know.'

'I wish you were a Maggie.'

'Well I'm not.'

Maggie, second year Chemistry student, believer in free love, had been Parker's previous girlfriend. As far as Parker was concerned the entire female world was now divided into those who were Maggies and those who were not.

'Who you keeping it for?'

'Not you.'

'It will wither and die.'

'I'll take that chance.'

He sat up chewing a grass blade and she recognised the lazy look in his eyes that led to argument.

She reached for her briefcase.

'I want some help with my Contracts.'

'Coward.'

'Seriously. I haven't understood a thing since the case of the Carbolic Smoke Ball.'

'You're a dim little cookie.'

She flicked through her notes.

'What's the problem?'

'Somebody buys a vase. It has a crack in and he doesn't notice.'

'*Caveat emptor.*'

'And one on the Statute of Limitations; and another where A has posted a letter and B hasn't received it and another where a man sells his house and the chap who buys it starts to decorate it before the contracts are signed then the first chap changes his mind about selling it because the second chap has made it look so good.'

He took the book from her.

'Why do you bother your beautiful head?'

Peach looked across the park. 'There's something about the Spring. I often think if I were blind I would still know it by its feel. It's tangible.'

'I like the Fall.'

'Too depressing; summer disintegrating.'

'It has majesty.'

'No promise.'

Parker was watching her.

'The cracked vase,' she said, taking out her pen.

'One day you will try me just too far.'

'What will happen?'

'You'll find it in the *News of the World*.'

Six

'It's all very well for you,' Peach said, taking a red dress from the cupboard, 'you don't have to go. "Tell me, Mr Higginbottom, how do you approach your hiatus hernias, through the chest or the abdomen?" "How are you, Miss Gatehouse? I do so admire your parents..."'

Sarah sat on the bed painting her fingernails green. 'Perhaps the son will be something.'

Peach pulled the dress over her head. 'Stuffed shirt,' she said into it. 'Professor Hopkins' Senior Registrar, MS at twenty-five; as if anybody cared.'

'Why do you bother?'

'Public relations. They send each other patients. Mustn't let a gall-bladder slip through the old fingers you know. Parker's picking me up after. We're going to Cleo's. What's that?'

'Sounds like the bell.'

'Be an angel. Anna-Maria's gone to Communion. It's the waiting-room.'

'I've only got seven green nails.'

'They don't look at your nails. I'm not decent.'

'What do I say?'

'No Surgery tonight, it's Thursday. If you can't cope I'll come.'

'I'm too good-natured.' Sarah drifted out, Lady Macbeth, hands spread-eagled.

No word still from Henry. Sarah knew nothing. Fleur was in Italy. Almost a fortnight. Obviously he wasn't interested. She struggled with the zip, arms behind her, couldn't quite reach, sat down at the dressing-table to do her face. It was going to be deadly at the Lindsays, paralysing…

She heard Sarah, who never hurried, take the stairs two at a time, urgently, watching her come in, in the mirror.

'A child with a razor-blade. There's blood everywhere.'

Always when everyone was out. Accidents and children vomiting in the waiting-room.

Peach stood up slowly.

'Wait, I'll zip you. There's a little hook at the top…'

'It doesn't matter.'

'Want me to come with?'

'Yes.'

It was Mrs Scutt who served in the local fruiterers.

'Razor-blade. Dunno how she got 'old of it.'

They stood there passively, the child wide-eyed in a grubby dress, while blood dripped from every finger onto the floor.

'The doctor's out,' Peach said.

Four eyes rested with faith on her own. This was the doctor's.

She backed away, stretched her mouth into a smile. 'I'll get a dressing. Won't be a moment. Clean it up. See if it needs stitching.' She escaped into the dispensary. The door opened after her.

'She's come over.'

Oh God. She sent Sarah for water and searched for gauze.

She put the child's head between its knees and the blood zig-zagged down her leg and onto her grey socks.

Sarah came back with Grant.

'Need any help?'

'Mrs Scutt. A razor-blade,' she said, with relief.

'Dunno 'ow she got 'old of it.' Mrs Scutt repeated her piece.

Grant took the child's hand. 'Let's have a look shall we?'

'I can't help it,' Peach said.

'Looked worse than it was.' Grant sat on the bed next to Sarah agitating the varnish bottle.

'Perhaps I can do the last two before there are any more alarums and excursions.'

'Didn't even need stitching.'

'Why can't they be more careful. Did you clean the floor?'

'Yes. Forget it. Going out?'

'I always dress up for Anna-Maria's goulash!'

'What's a ganglion?' Sarah said.

'Why?'

'Ronnie has one.'

'Where?'

'On his foot.'

'For God's sake!' Peach said.

In the taxi Peach thought where is my capacity for love; Christian love, suffering little children even if they were bloody. You would think that after all these years ... but it gets no better. Even as a child she had hated going into the surgery while it was Grant's favourite playground, sitting at the desk, buzzing for patients, handling forbidden instruments. Hers was always the role of patient in 'Let's play doctors.' She'd sit submissively while her leg was bandaged her stomach palpated or her blood pressure taken. When it was her turn to be the doctor she'd slide down from the couch. 'Let's play something else.'

She tried to keep apart; it wasn't always possible. The years were punctuated with doorstop emergencies, street accidents, severed fingers, telephone pleas for urgent help; the sick, the dead, the dying, the panic-stricken. She did what she had to, not with love. We are not all the same. I can't put out my hand.

Professor Lindsay had married well. In the master-suite the bed was frilled with ivory nylon, framed with gold cherubs whose brothers held the subdued lights patiently aloft, guarding the peach glass mirrors. Peach added her coat to the three fur wraps on the bed, thought of her mother's bedroom with its typewriter on the dressing-table, letters from hospitals on the mantel-piece, *Medical Journals* by the bed and shoes under everything.

'I'm so pleased you could come. I'm Anne Lindsay. I missed your mother's party. I was in Majorca, the weather was foul.' Peach hadn't heard her soft step on the carpet. She was a tall woman, uniformed in black, two rows of pearls, hair elegantly chignoned. 'We have a Young People's Aid to China,' she was saying, 'and Ian said he was sure you'd be interested. The first meeting is on Wednesday week. We hope to arrange a barbecue and a midnight matinee later in the summer, and perhaps a fete; Lord Moleham is a patient of Ian's and has promised his lawn...'

They were in the corridor and Peach thought of them at home eating Anna-Maria's goulash, or at Sarah's on the floor with Brie from Harrods and Beaujolais slightly sour because Sarah never remembered the cork.

At the drawing-room door she had a brief impression of a grand piano with photographs, curly-legged chairs and a lit portrait of Anne Lindsay over the fireplace.

'This is Peach Gatehouse, Hilda Hallam's daughter, you know; Marian Rothway, and this great fellow is Adrian from the West End Children's. His bark is worse than his bite, isn't it, Marion? And this is Greta West, she takes those lovely shiny photos for the Medical Journals, and husband, neurologist at Fulham, just back from the States and going to tell us about it, aren't you, Harry? And Ben and Atalanta David, psychiatrists from the Barrington. Ben writes those great big books. Ian of course you know. What about a drink for Peach, Ian?'

No sign of a son. With luck he was elsewhere, unforeseen circumstances...

'Ah, and this is my son.'

She turned to the doorway and it was filled by Henry, head almost touching the lintel.

She felt tired suddenly like some horrid joke wondered if he thought she'd dressed up in scarlet because she'd known, to kill, wanted to explain it was for Cleo's. He had on a dark suit, blue-striped tie, South-West London, of course, it had worried her at Sarah's.

'We've met.' He put out his hand.

'Have you really? I thought it would be

such a surprise.'

She couldn't believe the sensation was in her hand alone that he was unaware; everything was in her mind, the cherubs on Anne Lindsay's bed, the Scutt child with its bloody fingers, Sarah's green nails, it must have gone no further than her fingertips because he moved across the room to talk to Adrian Rothway; betrayed she sat down between Greta West and Atalanta David who made room for her on the sofa.

'Henry gets handsomer every day,' Greta West said, her melodious voice a surprise because she looked horsey and had a man's hands.

'Has been since he was a little boy. I always remember him in his coat with the velvet collar. You should have put him into films, Ian.'

'Be a great deal better paid,' Professor Lindsay said. 'Haw, haw, haw!'

'How are Elliot and Hilda?' Professor Lindsay said. He was holding a sherry glass with a colourless liquid in it. 'I'd like you to try this. *Specialité de la maison*.'

'They're fine, thank you.' She took the glass.

'Still rushing around like mad things? Never known such a couple for work.'

'Like mad things.'

Henry stood by the piano with his back to her.

She couldn't think why it hadn't occurred to her, not that there was any reason that it should have. Whatever it was they were talking about Adrian Rothway was interested, listening intently. This I know and know full well I do not like thee Doctor Fell. Yet she did. It made no difference. The back of his neck; she hadn't remembered noticing the furrow down the back of his neck.

'How is it?'

She looked up at Professor Lindsay.

'The drink?'

She supposed she had drunk it. There was a burning sensation in the region of her sternum.

'Can I get you another?'

'No. Thank you.'

'I know your mother,' Atalanta David said. 'She's a remarkable woman. But then of course you know.'

'Of course.' She must pull herself together or they would think she was some kind of moron. Why didn't somebody tell me, Fleur or Sarah. Sarah must have known. She turned her head away from the piano to Atalanta who was talking to her.

'...and your father must have one of the largest practices this side of the river. There doesn't seem to be a patient in London who hasn't at one time or another been through the hands of Elliot Gatehouse. He is the kindest of men. I suppose that's the answer.'

'Not the Medicine?' Greta said, leaning across Peach.

'Elliot loves his patients to the exclusion of all else.'

And I hate them to the exclusion of all else.

'He's a damned good doctor, though,' Professor Lindsay said. 'I remember in the old days, before your time of course,' he said to Peach, 'there wasn't a thing Elliot wouldn't tackle in that surgery of his, tonsillectomy, veins, the lot. He even excised an infected cyst on a monkey once. Has he still got that parrot of his that used to swear at all the patients?'

'Not any more,' Peach said, 'It died.'

The dog it was that died. She remembered the parrot, a vicious-looking red and green creature with blinking, beady eyes who lived in a corner of the surgery and from time to time told the patients to 'shut up and go home.'

'Henry has a marvellous record collection,' Anne Lindsay was saying and Peach realised she was saying it to her. 'You must get him to show it to you. I'm not a music lover, give me a good play with a strong plot but then of course we can never book up in advance, Ian's always busy at the last minute. I've taken to sneaking out to the odd matinee lately, it's the only way.'

They drifted in to dinner. In the dark green

dining-room they ate cheese soufflé to the use of Electro Convulsive Therapy in endogenous depression, duck with cherries while Adrian Rothway who sat next to her told her with enthusiasm of the original work he was engaged upon on haemorrhagic disease of the new born, and pineapple and kirsch to the extrinsic, intrinsic and hereditary causes of cancer. Professor Lindsay poured and eulogised upon the wine and his wife from the other end of the table kept up a ceaseless flow of chatter.

Peach found that her cheeks ached from smiling and her head from the strain of trying to concentrate on what Rothway was saying and at the same time to hear what Henry and Atalanta were talking about on the other side of the table.

I have to be everywhere always; on all sides.

'Shall we leave the men to their stories?' Anne said. 'Not too long now, Ian.'

Back in the drawing-room she poured coffee from an elegant silver pot and said sugar and cream and Peach wondered what she was doing there with Marian Rothway and Greta West and Atalanta David and Anne, women who knew exactly where they were going and were speaking of their various retreats in the country and how Greta's idea of bliss was to spend Saturday potting geraniums and Marion's to take brass rubbings in the local church and Atalanta confessed to whitewashing everything she could find with inhibition-releasing abandon and Anne said Oh no there was nothing like tapestry for the nerves she was doing a complete set of chair covers for the dining-room and had completed six out of the eight and she really must haul the men out or they would be there all night and anyway the coffee would be cold.

They came in with cigars looking pleased with themselves and a little sheepish and Professor Lindsay said 'Anne dear, the coffee's not terribly hot' and she said 'I'll get it heated' in such a way that Peach had the impression it was a dialogue indulged in many times before and it was part of a ritual.

Henry poured the liqueurs and they spoke of nuclear disarmament and the menace of Red China, then Anne said Henry dear why don't you take Peach inside to listen to some records and the nightmare was over.

You could see her influence in Henry's room; the royal blue bedcover matching the carpet, shaded curtains. In the bookcase were Cecil on Medicine, Eden and Holland's *Obstetrics*, Gaisford's *Paediatrics*.

There was a record player, wires over the floor, two speakers, a squash racquet in the corner, photograph, framed, of a rugger fifteen.

'Sorry about this,' Henry said. 'I had no idea it was going to be you. A girl, Mother said, so would I come for dinner. I live at the Hospital.'

'Sorry?'

'There's quite a covey of us here tonight. I know you hate it.'

He hadn't given her a thought since Sarah's. How one deceived oneself.

There was a flat-topped desk beneath the window. On it was a polished bone. Henry picked it up.

'This is the tibia of a middle-aged male. Bones are my speciality. Each time I've looked at once since that night at Sarah's all I could see was your face. It's been driving me crazy.'

'You left early.'

'I had to. There was an arthroplasty of the hip I was watching. I remembered your eyes blue.'

'Grey.'

He put the bone down and stood by the window. The curtains were the dark leaves of a plane tree.

'I represent everything you hate. That's why I didn't get in touch.' He nodded towards the door. 'If you don't want to get involved...'

It was two weeks too late.

'I love you,' Henry said.

'I thought...'

'Don't think. There's something I've been

wanting to do all evening.'

He came to her and fastened the hook Sarah had left at the top of her dress.

'This too.' He turned her round and kissed her.

'Nothing exists,' he said.

'Since Sarah's?'

'Always. All it needed was shape.'

'I've been so lonely.'

'You won't be.'

'There was a girl in the waiting-room,' Peach said, 'before I came out. She'd been playing with a razor-blade. There was blood all over the floor.'

He held her tightly.

'I felt no pain; I wasn't even sorry. Only disgust.'

'Poor darling.' He kissed her eyes.

'I didn't tell you for that. Only that I'm not a very nice person.'

'I prefer my own judgement.'

'It's true. I measure myself against Mother, Dad, Grant...'

'Peach, stop it.'

'I just wanted you to know...'

'Peach!'

'You see...'

His head blotted out the plane tree.

'You've been a long time,' Anne Lindsay said. 'What did you play?'

Peach looked at her horrified, then rea-

71

lised she meant records and turned to Henry for help, but Anne hadn't waited for an answer.

'I expect it was opera,' she said. 'The only one I can listen to is Strauss; at least he has a little tune one can remember. Henry's more on the heavy side, aren't you, Henry? I suppose one has to understand it.'

She sat through a battle over Wagner, Henry for, Adrian against, and thought there is so much to discover a whole world suddenly opened up, and told an interested Atalanta about her Law studies listening to her other self the real with Henry. Then Greta and Harry West said they must go and could they give her a lift and Anne said of course not Henry had the car outside and would take her home, won't you Henry? And Henry hesitated, teasing her, then said all right reluctantly.

Going down in the lift Peach said, 'The headless lady, you don't really think...?'

And Henry took her in his arms spoiling her hair and said: 'Yes but look what she's missing,' and they didn't realise they were on the ground floor until they heard someone rattling the iron trellis and Adrian Rothway's voice from high up bellowing 'Someone's left the ruddy gates open.'

Outside on the steps Henry said: 'The car's round the other side, if you wait here...'

But she didn't want him to leave her. 'I'll come with,' and then a voice from the court-yard said 'Baby!' and it was Parker waiting to take her to Cleo's.

Seven

'Cleo was expecting us,' Parker said, for the fourth time.

They sat on the college steps.

'I said I was sorry.'

'What's with this Henry?'

'I love him.'

'A sawbones? You'd run a mile.'

'In the wrong direction.'

'Baby, you always said…'

'This is love, not logic.'

'I waited an hour. Cleo was mad.'

'I said I was sorry.'

'…made me look pretty silly.'

'I completely forgot.'

'Must be some guy.' Parker stood up. She could see he was angry.

'Where are you going?'

'To find a Maggie.'

'Parker…'

She watched him thread his way through the sunbeamed tracery of beards and pony-tails, stretch-pants and saris, in the fore-court and disappear, hunch-shouldered, through the door to the Union.

She hated to hurt people. Last night Parker had been hurt. The three of them had stood

74

for a moment immobilised by surprise on the steps of the flats where Henry lived. Peach had been the first to recover. She had a headache, she told Parker, Cleo would have to excuse her, Henry was taking her home.

In the blackness of the car park Henry said: 'Who is he?'

'A friend from College.'

'You knew he'd be there?'

'I forgot.'

'Have you a headache?'

'No.'

'Why did you tell him you had?'

'I didn't want to go to Cleo's. I told you I'm not a nice person.'

'You asked him to pick you up here?'

'I didn't know it was going to be you. It was a duty dinner. Mother insisted.'

'I should insist you go with Parker. We could catch him up.'

'He's angry. Probably gone to find a Maggie.'

'A what?'

'Nothing. Just an expression.'

Henry's hands were in his pockets. 'I know nothing about you. What makes you tick, if you love Parker. I love you. I have to go from there.'

'It was your fault I forgot about Parker.'

Parker had shattered the evening.

'I hate to hurt people.'

Henry put his arm round her. 'This is

going to be some love.'

The evening began to mend.

'What's up with Parker?' Sarah said, sitting down on the steps and spreading her duffel coat over her knees.

'He looks like the wrath of God.'

'He's angry about Cleo's. I completely forgot. Why didn't you tell me about Henry?'

'I didn't know what do for the best. Fleur told me he was at the South-West London. It had to be you of all people. I didn't realise he was the Professor's son. Can't you pretend he's a taxi-driver or a bricklayer? Don't think about it.'

'I don't. Did you know he won a gold medal for his Finals and the Fortescue prize for pathology? Grant told me ... what's funny?'

'You'd think no one had ever been in love.'

'Sorry if I'm boring you.'

'You aren't, darling. I have something crashingly boring to tell you, though.' Sarah lit a cigarette and drew on it, tilting her head back and exhaling through her nose. 'I'm in the cart.'

'Sarah!'

'It was Ronnie's fault. He's so abysmally careless.'

'What will you do?'

'Ronnie has a friend who has a friend. It's all terribly sterile and outrageously expensive.'

'Sarah you can't!'

'Honey-bunch I have no alternative.'

'It's an offence, apart from being dangerous. You know that.'

'This particular criminal is highly recommended and they've assured me the risk is nil. I have to do something.'

'Let me think.'

'I've thought darling. Besides which it's all fixed. That's why I didn't tell you before. I knew you wouldn't like it.'

'Is Ronnie going with you?'

Sarah shook her head. 'You know Ronnie.'

'I'll come then.'

'I'll be all right alone.'

'When is it?'

'Thursday.'

'I don't like it,' Peach said.

'*I'm* not exactly thrilled to bits.'

Grant walked along Belsize Park in the fading light and argued with himself the wisdom of his decision. For the past week he had telephoned, written, called at the hospital, but Lesley Marshall would have nothing to do with him. 'I'm sorry, Grant! I just don't go out with people.' 'Sorry, Grant, the rest of the day I devote to Veronica.' 'Grant, why don't you forget it? You're wasting your time, honestly you are.' 'Grant, there are so many girls who'd be only too pleased...' But there was only one that he wanted, one with green eyes, red hair, white skin the thought of which kept him tossing and turning at nights.

The porter at the hospital had given him her address.

The evening pavements were quiet. What was she doing, would she be angry with him? It was a bit of a nerve really but he had to do something. He hadn't even an excuse. I've brought your book back. But there was no book. I was just passing so I thought... Perhaps some flowers. He looked vaguely around but the shops were shut. Only a man with one arm selling newspapers. I was just passing so I thought I'd bring you the evening paper. He stopped outside the house, three storeys behind a high brick wall, his courage failing just a little. The pathway was a mosaic of coloured tiles, mostly broken; in the garden a single laurel bush looked healthy among the debris. The stone steps were worn, dirty, the balustrade flaking. There were three white cards by the door with its leaded lights. Flat 1, Mrs Harcourt-Smith; Flat 2, Colonel Blair; Flat 3, Dr Lesley Marshall.

With each floor his resolution faded more. At the top his feet were dragging and he had almost decided upon the nearest newsreel in an effort to forget when he had a clear image of her rounded arms, white teeth... He rang the bell.

She was wearing a grey pleated skirt and a

black jumper and was in her stockinged feet. In her hand was a child's dress. She was surprised.

They stared at each other.

'I had to come,' Grant said. 'I had to.'

She looked at the floor seeming to think then stepped back and opened the door wider.

'I was letting down one of Veronica's dresses. She grows so fast.'

There was mimosa in the little hall, yellow, fluffy.

'It only lasts a day. I never can resist it. It reminds me of ... things.'

The sofa was littered with her sewing. Another dress, a white cotton sock, Clydella pyjamas. Her supper dishes were on a tray on the floor. She was listening to a radio play, which she turned off.

'Don't turn it off for me.'

She shrugged. 'It wasn't terribly interesting. I usually listen.'

The room was large, bright, comfortable. There was a snakes and ladders board on the table, a doll with no hair, evidence of love.

She curled up where she had been sitting on the sofa and tucked her feet beneath her, putting pins into the hem of the dress.

Grant stood by the fireplace. On the mantelpiece were notices of lectures, a lipstick, a toy watch on an elastic band, a wedding photo, Lesley, her hair longer then, smiling up at a pleasant-faced man.

'Graham,' Lesley said. 'That was his name.'

She searched for the tape-measure. 'We were married for six years. They were good years. Not perfect, nothing ever is except in retrospect. Just very happy. He was the Consultant Paediatrician at Luke's. That was how we met.'

'How long have you been on your own?'

'Just over a year.'

'Too long.'

'Veronica was four.'

She started sewing again, red-head bent. In the silence he heard the clock ticking. From all the speeches he had prepared in his mind he could bring forth nothing to say.

'I think I'll go,' he said finally. 'It was stupid of me to come. To imagine…'

She took a pin from her mouth and smiled. She was more beautiful than the image he had been carrying of her.

'I'm glad you came. It gets lonely after Veronica's gone to bed.'

He sat down on the edge of the armchair. 'I've been asking you for weeks.'

'I know you have. Each time you telephoned I've weakened just a little.'

She put down the sewing and her face became very still.

'Have you ever thought what's it like to be a widow? When Graham was alive we had quite a circle of friends, married couples like ourselves and the odd bachelor friends of Graham's. We entertained quite a bit, nothing formal, most of us were working. After he died things were different. The married friends invited me but I hated to go. They were kind but it was a strain on both sides because I was always the "odd man out" as it were. I couldn't stand the intimacy, the affectionate hand, the understanding glance, the innuendoes of marriage so unimportant to those who can share them. There was no longer anyone to finish *my* sentences, share *my* jokes, to know when I was sad, happy, sick, depressed, worried, just by looking at my face. I started refusing the invitations because I was happier alone. It wasn't that they flaunted their marriages, far from it, it was just that I seemed always to tangle with invisible marital chains. With the unmarried men it was worse. When Graham was ill they used to come up here to keep me company; we talked, sometimes late into the night, had coffee. As soon as he was dead the atmosphere was different, awkward; sex rearing its head where it wasn't wanted.'

She looked straight at him. 'That was difficult, too, at times. It's well known that the young widow is fair game. I know why.

There have been times when I've felt like going out into the street and grabbing the nearest man. I've been that desperate. I made up my mind then that the best way was to get involved in my work and in Veronica and leave any social contacts until I felt more ... detached. Your Mother's party was one of the exceptions... I couldn't very well refuse.'

'There are things in people's lives that no one dreams of,' Grant said. 'Not just the obvious things but the battles one has to do with one's soul.'

She took up the sewing again. 'Occasionally in the evenings I think I shall go crazy. Out of the window I watch the people hurrying to persons, places I know nothing about and I get the impression the entire world is going somewhere and that I have been forgotten, left on a ledge to rot. I have to stop myself from calling out to be taken with.'

'Whenever I've seen you you've been smiling,' Grant said.

'Loneliness has no face.'

Afterwards, and many times after that, Grant asked himself what they had talked about. Before he realised the sewing was finished and they had drunk coffee which he had helped her make and laughed over the dishes which he never had to do at home and had his feet up on the footstool and it was almost midnight. When she spoke her green eyes widened and narrowed, taking their cue from what she said. When she moved her movements were natural, fluid. She had slim ankles and high breasts, a long slender neck.

He watched her put on her shoes and tidy away the sewing and lay the table for breakfast. Veronica had a serviette ring with a sailor on it.

In the little hall the mimosa was shrivelled, dead. He kissed her forehead and said: 'May I come again?'

She stood quite still, saying nothing.

'Lesley,' he said into the green eyes. 'I promise you can trust me.'

She put a cool hand against the side of his face.

'It isn't you I'm worried about, Grant; it's myself.'

Eight

'Are you sure,' Ronnie said, 'you don't want me to come with you?'

'I've told you. Peach is coming. You'd only be in the way.'

They were in bed. Sarah on her tummy, her face buried in the pillow. Ronnie sat beside her, knees drawn up, smoking.

'I'll be glad when it's tonight.'

'I'll be all right.'

'Moira was all right. Fine, Skipper said; right as rain. What shall I do?'

'About what?'

'Today. What shall I do?'

'Aren't you going to school?'

'It seems wrong somehow. Graphic Design and Lettering this morning. Perspective this afternoon... I suppose I may as well. You worried, Sarah?'

'I can think of pleasanter ways to spend a Thursday.'

'Moira was back at work in a couple of days. She was absolutely fine, Skipper said. I don't want you to worry, Sally.'

He called her Sally when they made love. She turned onto her back and watched him. He got out of bed and stood naked by the dressing-table putting out his cigarette. He had a white slim body. He put on his pants, made a boxer's pass at himself in the mirror, then pulled on his black denims from the chair. He zipped them with one hand and reached for his sweater with the other. He sat on the bed to put on his shoes and socks. When he was ready he opened the thin curtains and went out of the room.

Sarah lay watching the morning feet through the barred windows. Among the blacks and browns of the men there was a rash of beige and white high heels, few umbrellas. The day was going to be promising as far as the weather was concerned. Ronnie never got up first. Often he was still asleep, hidden by the bedclothes as he always slept, when she left for College.

The feet clip-clopped, sometimes four in line, empty shopping bags, briefcases, pinstripes. She had a sudden vision of the beach at home in Wales, miles and miles with nobody on it except herself, barefoot, nine years old, hair flying deliciously in the wind. She could feel the sand giving beneath her toes, the spray on her face, could smell the seaweed. Even at nine there had been boys. Roger and Stephen from the village throwing eternal stones into the sea and sticks for Tammy who was Stephen's dog to retrieve.

'I bet he's the fastest swimmer in Merioneth.'

'Bet I am.'

'Dog, I meant Sarah.'

'Bet I'm faster anyway, Stephen.'

'Bet you're not.'

'Bet I am.'

'Bet you're not.'

'Throw a stick then. No. Wait a minute.' She took off her dress and threw it on the sand, the cold morning wind making goose pimples on her chest. She looked about but there was no one to be seen on the beach or over the dunes except for herself and the two boys and Tammy panting, bedraggled, waiting for the next throw.

'Are you ready then?'

Sarah nodded standing by Tammy's nose.

'Off you go then!'

The stick whirled and the sea was icy round her ankles then biting at her stomach then she was swimming in the greyness as fast as she could watching Tammy from the corner of her eye swimming alongside. She reached the stick first but only just because she could stretch out her arm and she held it aloft for the boys to see then gave it to Tammy to fetch in.

'You see!' She was blue, shivering.

They'd lost interest. She dried herself on her dress then put it on. Tammy shook himself making her wet again.

'Race you to the big rock,' Roger said and they were off, laughing, Tammy alongside.

She had never been afraid, not of the physical things and not of the unpleasant.

'Who threw loganberries on Colonel Beater's French windows?'

'I did, Father.'

'Go and apologise then and when you return I'll have a word with you.'

Colonel Beater had been furious; had given her a bucket and a cloth and stood by while she cleaned up the mess that still oozed and dripped down onto his terrace. He called her all manner of names, scarlet with rage, but she was unrepentant, wondering only as she wrung her cloth out repeatedly, whether he would actually go off pop.

'You must have respect,' her father said, 'for other people's property, Sarah, it is terribly important.' Even when he was angry he did not raise his voice. He had the looks of a matinee idol and was making his steady way up the legal ladder, swaying a courtroom with his soft-spoken argument, his words becoming quieter as he developed his case, until the silence was tangible, suspending every quiet syllable, like fruit in a jelly.

Her mother had died when Sarah was seven. There were photographs of her all over the house, a plump woman, smiling; only at moments did Sarah remember her.

'She was very beautiful,' her father said and Sarah understood he meant like the blue mountains he loved and the valleys through which he walked in his leisure time and not like the cover of a glossy magazine.

She had been brought up, what bringing up there was, by Barnaby who really was Mrs Barnaby, who had been their house-keeper when her mother died and who had a hairy mole on her cheek and spoke little, getting on with her work and doing what she had to for Sir who was now 'his Wor-ship' and for Sarah whom she loved.

They were a quiet house, not getting in each other's way and needing not to make too much adjustment when Sarah came to London.

'I brought you some breakfast,' Ronnie said.

Sarah opened her eyes which had drifted shut. He stood by the bed, a cup in one hand with a spoon in it and a plate in the other.

'Thanks, Ronnie.'

She sat up and took them from him and he stood on like a small boy. It was the first time he had brought her as much as a glass of water.

'Is it alright? There wasn't much Nescafé.'

'I'll get a new one.'

'Not much sugar either.'

'It's fine.'

He went to the dressing-table and opened the top drawer.

'There's the money.'

'I know.'

He took his duffel coat from the bed where he'd spread it for extra warmth in the night.

'Think I'll go then.'

She drank the watery coffee.

'You'll be all right. Moira was fine.' He stood by the door a moment fiddling with the toggle on his coat.

He came over and kissed her.

'Skipper said it was nothing at all. Moira told him.'

She wished he would go.

'I'll see you tonight. Don't worry about the coffee. I'll get it.'

'All right Ronnie.'

'You're sure now?'

'Sure.' She smiled and he was gone, shutting the door with consideration as if she was ill.

In a moment he was back.

'I'll fetch the sugar too.'

'All right.'

'See you tonight.'

Peach walked up Harley Street glancing as she passed at the names on the brass plates. Many of them she had met in person at the dinner table, at home; many more were names familiar in family conversation. She looked up at the tall buildings. Several of them to a house, although it hadn't always been like that, and imagined them sitting at their desks, beautifully dressed in their white collars dispensing judgements. 'You to live,

89

and you to die; you to have it out; you for X-ray; you for another opinion. Mrs Galbraith's notes Nurse she appears to be going rapidly downhill and see if you can get me two stalls for the Comedy tonight and a nice table at the Coq d'Argent.' Listened to and judged upon they were disgorged into the street. A girl in a red coat, a woman in mink, face like a rat-trap beneath floral hat, a man with a schoolboy; it was impossible to tell whether they had had a tooth drilled or been handed a thin prognosis. One stood on a step; another was admitted; a white coat and a bright smile, 'Weather's a little better, yes…' 'Good morning Mrs Whitley…' 'Do come in, I'm sorry Doctor's been delayed…' 'Goodbye Mrs Crabtree, Major, goodbye.'

She pictured the waiting-rooms, gloomy witnesses of a bygone era whose heavy tables had not been fashioned for a handful of light-weight magazines and fireplaces that had been built for more than the odd fern or single bar electric stove.

'Mr Watson is ready for you now.' Great doors opening for nervous women with anxiety; staircases which had seen elegance, carrying men with piles.

Dr Bridges
Dr Alexander
Miss Hallam
Mr George St Clair

Peach rang the bell.

Miss Ivey had orange hair and lived in Balham and had been with her mother for twenty years.

'Hallo Miss Gatehouse, were we expecting you?' When she closed her mouth the upper teeth were still in evidence. As children she and Grant had played 'Miss Ivey'.

'No. I just wanted a word with Mother.'

'I'll slip you up between patients. We've a hectic morning and we're operating at one. We'll only have time for a sandwich.'

'I'll wait,' Peach said.

'In my office if you like.'

The teacup and the packet of Marie biscuits and 'Mother' framed. Another Miss Ivey only older and with grey hair and the unfortunate dental arrangement happily disappeared with time.

'I'll just sit here.' Peach indicated the bench in the hall.

'I hope we won't be long.'

Peach looked at her watch and sat down. She didn't really know why she had come at all only that she was nervous, nervous for Sarah who seemed to think no more of it than going to buy a hat only of course Sarah never wore hats, stupid comparison really. She'd promised to meet her at the Tottenham Court Road Station bookstall at twelve. It was on a whim really that she'd come. She'd half-slept all night worrying about Sarah; not that her mother could do anything she knew except deliver Sarah's baby for her, which Sarah didn't want. With the morning light she had decided that her mother was the person to discuss it with and that something should really be done, rather than allow Sarah to proceed with an unpleasant operation performed by a person of dubious competence.

Having made up her mind Peach had hurried downstairs only to discover that she had overslept and that her mother had already left for Harley Street. She was partly inclined to make no further effort but her conscience insisted with small promptings during the morning until the step had been taken.

A grey-haired man in a city suit with a red carnation in his buttonhole crossed the hall, looked at her for a moment then was gone through the front door.

What exactly was she going to say. Although this was probably easier than many of the thousand and one problems that had cropped up during her childhood and with which her mother was quite incapable of dealing.

'I'm one of the fairies in *Midsummer Night's Dream*. Will you make me a costume? It has to be green with wings at the back, not too large the stage isn't very big just wings...'You might as well ask her to build a bridge across the Thames; there was only one kind of sewing she could do and that with sutures. 'It's Prize-giving on Wednesday will you come?' 'Wednesday's impossible Peach I have my ante-natal at New Cross.' As if the School Governors should have known. 'I need a press for my tennis racquet, a tunic made for Greek dancing and a wreath for my hair. Can you come to Sports Day on the twelfth and the Swimming Gala at the end of June and Miss Fitzherbert says any mothers who can help with the teas on Parents' Day...' Even by stretching her imagination Peach had not been able to picture her mother together with the more conventional ones in a flowered hat attending the urn behind a trestle table. Throughout her childhood she had built up in her mind an image of the mother she would like to have produced for inspection on public occasions. She was conglomeration of the mothers of all her friends rolled into a glamorous one. The first thing one would notice about her was her smell; the heady, expensive, luxurious smell of scent which hinted at comfortable cuddles in a warm embrace. Then her smile; wide, rather like a film star's, revealing sparkling teeth. She would be tall, beautifully dressed, though not too ostentatious, and she would be surrounded by adoring children who clustered round her in the evenings while she patiently sewed name tapes onto countless garments (still in her lovely clothes) and created exotic confections in the twinkling of an eye for school plays or for fancy-dress. This paragon, in addition, would have acres and acres of time at her disposal to hear poems, no matter how many verses long, to listen to essays, both History and English, and have sufficient intelligence to know, having digested the data that the angle at B was forty-five degrees and the angle at C was eighty-nine degrees, what was the length of CD in centimeters to the nearest decimal point; and whether it was 'le' or 'la' pomme de terre. She would also accompany one to the dentist in the approved manner (instead of ringing one of her pals and saying do you mind having a look at Peach, George, you don't mind if she comes by herself do you and how is that impacted wisdom I sent you getting along), to buy house-shoes, and would sit patiently by the wall in the draughty hall where every Tuesday to the accompaniment of Miss Horne on the piano one executed one's *pas de chats*.

That the other girls envied her her unusual mother, Peach knew. She kept to herself the fact that each day brought problems that made her wish she was a little less extraordinary. Now her schooldays were over. Miss Fitzherbert had told her in the privacy of her study that she had parents who had set her a great example and that she hoped she, Peach, would make every effort to live up to the example she had been shown. She was now no longer dependent upon her mother for the numerous small services she had throughout childhood found so difficult to perform but she was still no closer to her than she ever had been. Like strangers they were always polite to each other, there was rarely, as between strangers, a clash of wills.

A girl well-advanced in pregnancy came heavily down the stairs.

'You can slip up now,' Miss Ivey said, popping out from her cubby hole.

Sarah, Peach thought, and remembered why she had come.

The consulting room was pleasantly comfortable, with heavy furniture and a Persian carpet that had belonged to Hilda's mother and was well worn.

She was standing by the desk, her back to Peach and speaking into the telephone. Sunlight filtered through the window and picked out her sensible shoes in its beam. She wore a navy-blue suit slightly shiny at the back and you could just see the collar of her pale-blue crêpe blouse beneath the short, grey hair.

'Yes, yes,' she was saying, 'yes.' With her

free hand she opened a desk drawer and removed her handbag.

'Look,' she said. 'Take her down to the theatre and get the forceps ready. No, don't give her anything else, ring up Dr Dixon and he'll see to that. Tell him I'll be over in three minutes.'

She put the receiver down and was almost at the door before she saw Peach.

'Look, tell Miss Ivey there's a panic on at Adelaide's and to cancel everyone. She can ring me there.'

She was halfway down the curving staircase when Peach heard her call:

'Peach.'

Peach looked over the banister.

'Did you want me?'

'Yes. No. It doesn't matter.'

'Must rush. See you tonight.'

The door slammed and she was gone.

From the window of the consulting room Peach watched Mann rouse himself from his doze and nose his way into the traffic.

There was a silver vase with early roses on her mother's desk, a portrait of Elliot as a young man, a paper-knife, notes on Mrs Glen-Bott a reminder to 'follow up Anne Green.'

For the patients there was time.

She went down to give the message to Miss Ivey.

Nine

'Where's Ronnie?' Sarah said for the hundredth time.

Peach put the glass of water on a chair next to the bed and said: 'He'll be here soon.'

'He finishes at five. He should have been home hours ago.'

Peach sighed and sat down on a cushion in the corner. It had been a long day.

She'd waited by the bookstall at Tottenham Court Road Station while a complete batch of early edition evening newspapers had arrived and been sold and had just decided with relief that Sarah had changed her mind when she appeared. She was holding a white carrier with 'Floride (Modes)' printed on it.

'I hoped you weren't coming.'

'I bought a dress. It was in the window.'

At a time like this. 'Sarah, don't let's go.'

'Green Tricel. Great for the summer; drip-dry.'

Sarah walked towards the booking office. 'I spent three of the witch's pounds.' She took out her purse. 'Look, I told you, you don't have to come with.'

In the train there was one free seat. Sarah sat down, the carrier bag on her lap and Peach stood by her knees.

'I had a letter from my father,' Sarah said. 'He's coming to London for Grand Night at his Inn. He hates leaving his garden at this time of year.'

'When?'

Her answer was lost as the train clattered through a tunnel enclosing them in sound.

The address was in Notting Hill Gate. The street they walked along became progressively depressing. Peach wanted to turn back.

'Go ahead,' Sarah said. 'I'll be all right.'

But it was for Sarah that she was anxious.

A woman in a mauve lace-knit jumper and fur-trimmed slippers opened the door. She eyed them quickly.

'Third floor!' she said and went back to her bolt-hole.

The 'nurse', a middle-aged woman in a grey-white nylon coat, was angry about the money. Peach found thirty shillings in her wallet and Sarah promised faithfully to send the rest before the end of the week.

The woman took Sarah away and Peach sat for a long while on the edge of an un-savoury looking armchair and looked at the grimy red piece of carpet and the ugly fireplace with the clock that had stopped and the ash-tray that said 'Watneys' and the table covered with soiled green plush and a torn copy of *Woman* three years old and the linoleum fraying at the seams. Then she stood up and looked through the grimy window over the half-nets out into the quiet street where black faces passed spasmodically by.

She heard a sound and spun round but it was only the 'Floride (Modes)' bag sliding onto the floor from the wall against which Sarah had propped it.

After a while Sarah came back propelled by the Nurse.

'Are you all right?' Peach said.

The nurse said: 'Of course she is. Right as rain.'

'Is there anywhere we can get a taxi?' She should have thought of it before.

'Station.'

'Can you manage that?' she asked Sarah.

''Course she can. Don't forget the money.'

'Thank you,' Sarah said and put a cigarette in her mouth, her hand trembling as she held the match.

'All right, Sarah?' Peach said from the floor. It was getting dark and her limbs ached from the cramped position.

'I wish Ronnie would come. You know what I thought of, while the witch was doing it I mean?'

'What did she look like?'

'A little Central European with tired eyes.

It's a trick! I try at the dentist's; concentrate on something completely different and before you know where you are it's all over.'

'What did you think of?'

'Rats. We used to keep chickens at home, I mean in Wales, we don't any more, Barnaby's too old to look after them. From time to time there'd be an outbreak of rats, they'd come running along the back of the garden. When they got bad we used to borrow Stephen's dog and send him after them. He was a beautiful ratter. It was quite an occasion and all the kids would come to watch. We'd put Tammy on the bank behind the henhouse and a soon as he started sniffing and scratching we'd all dig like mad in the direction he wanted to go. Sometimes we had to go quite deep but he never made a mistake. He'd get more and more excited until he'd snap his teeth and "whoops" there you were. He never ate them of course, just nipped them in the throat and stood back panting while we took it away with a fork. By the end of the afternoon we'd have eight or nine little grey corpses...' She stopped abruptly.

'Sarah?'

Sarah's eyes were wide with horror.

'Peach, quickly. Something's happened!'

Peach scrambled up and pulled back the bedclothes.

'Sarah! Oh my God!'

She opened the door of the bedroom and with relief saw Ronnie leaning against the front door.

'Quick,' she said, 'get a doctor. Sarah's had a haemorrhage. No, you stay with her. I'll ring Mother, ask her what to do.'

He stood where he was.

'For God's sake move, Ronnie. This is serious.'

Ronnie stared at her, then took a tin from his pocket.

'I brought the coffee. Sarah wanted coffee. But I forgot the sugar.' He started to cry. 'I forgot the sugar.'

'Oh no! You're drunk!'

'Poor Ronnie's bloody drunk and he forgot the sugar...'

She pulled him away from the door by his coat. He raised an arm.

'What the hell you think you're doing...'

'Go in to Sarah,' she said. 'No, don't... I'll be back.'

There was a call-box at the end of the street. A youth in high boots was inside lolling against the panes and looking at himself in the little mirror as he spoke into the receiver.

Peach tapped on the door.

He took no notice so she opened it.

'Can't you bloody wait?'

'Sorry. It's terribly urgent. I have to get a

101

doctor quickly.'

'Or-right. Look Jack,' he said into the telephone, 'Gotta take a powder. See you.'

Everything seemed to take an age. Two of the pennies slid through into the returned coins and she had to put them in again. The bell rang leisurely.

'Hallo, Mother? No, I'm all right, it's Sarah. Look she's going to have a baby, at least she was, and she's bleeding like mad and collapsed. What shall I do? No, only me and Ronnie, that's Sarah's friend, but he's drunk anyway. Will you? Thanks awfully. Twenty-nine. The basement.'

She ran all the way back.

Ronnie was sitting on the floor in the hall.

'Mother's sending an ambulance. She'll meet us at the hospital.'

'Don't tell Sarah I forgot the sugar,' Ronnie said.

'Who was that?' Elliot said.

Hilda was dialling. 'Peach. Sarah's aborting.'

'Sarah?'

Hilda nodded.

'She been trying to get rid of it?' Elliot said.

'Apparently, silly girl. I'm taking her in.'

'Is Peach in the midst of it all?'

'Presumably.'

'She'll hate that. Did you know Sarah was

in trouble?'

'We'd be the last to know.'

'Until it comes to picking up the pieces.'

'Hallo, I want an ambulance...'

Elliot stood up. 'I'll take you down.'

'Where are they taking her?' Ronnie said as the ambulance men negotiated the narrow hall with Sarah on a stretcher. 'Where are they taking my Sally?'

'Queen Adelaide's,' Peach said. 'She's very ill.'

Ronnie stood up, supporting himself against the wall. His eyes were red-rimmed.

'Is she going to die?'

'Of course not. Mother's going to look after her.'

'Skipper said it would be all right. He said it would be. I'll murder the bastard.'

He lurched up the stairs behind her.

'Where are they taking her?'

'I told you. Queen Adelaide's.'

A few passers-by stared inside the lighted ambulance.

Peach went up the three steep steps and Ronnie tried to follow.

'You a relative, Sir?' the ambulance man said.

'He's drunk.' Peach said.

'Like hell I am.' Ronnie stuck out his chin.

'Sorry Sir.' The ambulance man took his arm and tried to pull him off the step.

Ronnie put up his fists.

'Ronnie, please!' Peach said.

A man in a cloth cap who had been watching took hold of Ronnie's shoulders and pulled him onto the pavement. Ronnie resisted for a moment, swearing, then sat down suddenly on the kerb and began to cry.

The ambulance man pulled up the steps and shut the doors.

Peach watched Sarah's white face and swayed to the urgent bell.

'Tea?' Sister Bright said, crackling into her office. 'Horlicks?'

'No thank you,' Elliot said.

'What about your daughter?'

'I won't thank you,' Peach said. 'Nothing at all.'

They sat on either side of the gas-fire which was turned low and hissing.

'I can't understand how you let her,' Elliot said. 'You know that it's both criminal and dangerous, even if Sarah didn't.'

'I tried to stop her. You don't know Sarah.'

'Who did it?'

'Some loathsome woman in Notting Hill Gate.'

'You must be out of your mind.'

'I told you, Sarah wouldn't listen. How long will they be?'

Elliot looked at his watch. 'They've been

in the theatre some time. Should be any minute. Sarah's a bit fast, isn't she?'

Peach smiled.

'What's so funny?'

'"Fast". It's so old-fashioned.'

'The choice of word is unimportant. You know what I mean.'

'Perhaps. It's her own business.'

'There seem to be others involved just at present. No man is an island,' Elliot said.

'Let he who is guiltless cast the first stone. Since we are quoting.'

'No one is casting stones, Peach.'

'You were.'

'I was commenting.'

'You were insinuating. Everyone has a right to do what he wants.'

Elliot said nothing.

'Well, hasn't he?'

'Has he, Peach?'

Peach stared into the fire. 'I'm not going to get involved. Your generation makes everything so complicated. Life is different now, there is more at stake.'

'There has always been the same. It is you who have changed. You and Sarah and Ronnie, the lot of you. You're looking through the wrong end of the telescope.'

They were quiet for a while then Peach said:

'There was a man on the platform the other day when I was going to College. He was just

105

standing there reading his newspaper when quite suddenly he felt flat and started writhing around all over the place foaming at the mouth.'

'Sounds like an epileptic.'

'It was revolting. Out of the whole length of the platform he had to be standing next to me.'

'It's like a sore finger,' Elliot said, 'everyone seems to knock it. They don't really. It only appears that way because it's sensitive.'

Peach leaned across and pushed back his cuff.

'It seems awfully long. Shouldn't Mother be down?'

Hilda came in calmly as if to breakfast or dinner.

'Sarah?' Peach said.

'She's lost a lot of blood but she'll be all right. It was a bit tricky before we got the transfusion going.'

'Thank goodness you were at home when I phoned.'

'It would have been a lot more sensible if I'd known about it before,' Hilda said. 'Why didn't you tell me?'

'I tried to, this morning,' Peach said. 'In Harley Street.'

Hilda looked at her, mentally winding the film of the day's events backwards until she came to the spot where Peach was standing in her consulting room. 'I'd forgotten,' she said. 'So you did.'

Ten

'In our day,' Hilda said, taking off her mask and hat in the Surgeon's Room, 'one was expected to come to one's marriage a virgin.'

Amy was tying up her rubber operating apron.

'A complete trans-valuation of values appears to have taken place,' Hilda went on. 'We were living in the Dark Ages. These apparently are the light, or should I say enlightened. There is not only no stigma attached to loss of virginity but it is also tolerably in order and not uncommon to carry a pregnancy to the altar. I can't pretend to understand.'

'There is another phenomenon of the age,' Amy said, putting her feet into rubber boots. 'The trial marriage. In our day it was "don't squeeze me till I'm yours" like they put on the tomatoes. I suppose that was what Sarah was up to.'

'Trial marriage my foot! She hasn't the slightest intention of getting married. When I was taking her BP today I said "I suppose you and Ronnie are going to get married soon", you can't get a word out of Peach.

Sarah looked at me as if I had suggested something quite obscene. She said: "Can you imagine trying to digest Torts and Contracts with a screaming baby, a line of washing over your head and a husband waiting for his dinner?" I'm not certain about the terms of reference anyway. What happens during this trial marriage if the girl turns out to be hopeless in bed? Is she condemned to a life of spinsterhood for want of a little patience and understanding?'

Hilda took her skirt from the hanger. 'And there's another thing; the "trial" seems only to apply to the physical side of things. I haven't noticed them putting such qualities as devotion, unselfishness, good-humour and tolerance to any test, not to mention such highly desirable attributes as ability to wash, albeit by machinery, cook, clean, sew and generally provide for a family. It does seem just a little unfair.'

'I once saw a film,' Amy said, picking up a mask, 'in which the mother walks into the room of her son whose marriage is on the point of breaking up. She thumps an angry and indicative hand on the double bed. "If a marriage is on the rocks," she says, the accent of course is American, I was never a good mimic, "the rocks are right there!" She may of course be right but it is often possible to get rid of the rocks by tactful application of some of the qualities you've already mentioned, in particular understanding. Today the thing to do seems to be to pick up your rocks and cart them off to a different bed, or beds, ad infinitum, until you are sick and tired or perhaps by that time too old to lug them any further, preferring to lie on them. The trouble with us, Hilda, is that we are no longer "with it".'

'Since to be "with it",' Hilda said, 'you have apparently to be cruel, dirty, untidy, unpunctual, noisy, arrogant, rude, extravagant, immodest, immoral, drunk, ignorant…'

'I get the general idea,' Amy said.

'…I can't say it worries me unduly. Possibly our own standards in today's light are not particularly desirable. I don't know. I only know that the more young people I meet, the more I talk to, the older I feel. Sometimes I think I am Father Time himself; I feel that remote.' She glanced at the wall clock and fastened her blouse. 'I now have to go down and be thanked by Sarah's father for picking up the pieces.'

'I rather liked Sarah when I met her at your place.'

'Sarah's all right, none of those horrible things I mentioned except of course unchaste. She's Peach's closest ally.'

'I have a ventrisuspension waiting for me on the table,' Amy said into her mask. 'I'd better get on. I wish you the best of luck with Dad.'

On the floor below, Peach found a man with grey hair sitting by Sarah's bed.

'This is my father, Peach.'

What did one call a Judge?

He stood up. He was wearing a black jacket and striped trousers.

'Sarah's told me about you.' He was very soft-spoken, like Sarah. 'She owes her life to you and your mother. I am grateful. She's all I have.'

'And your garden,' Sarah said.

Peach sat on the end of the bed.

'That behaves...' He raised an eyebrow at Sarah. 'I've planted some very fine Arab Queens, large cactus, you know and have filled the bed beneath the south wall with Mary Richards and Chorus Girl...'

'He's talking about dahlias,' Sarah said.

'...I am indeed, this is not my chrysanthemum year. I was discouraged by my incurves; mind you, though, my yellow Arthur Billitts were second to none in the early flowerings, though I say it myself. I'll feel more kindly disposed towards them next year I shouldn't doubt.' He pulled a gold watch from his waistcoat. 'Sarah girl, I have to go. I've to see Mrs Gatehouse and then pay a visit or two before tonight. The dinner will be deadly dull and murderous for my ulcer for I've no willpower, but I came all the way from Aberllan to attend it and attend it

I must.'

He looked at the flowers next to the bed. 'There was a man outside selling Fosteriana Cantata but they were very poor specimens indeed, very poor. I'll put a cheque in the post. Don't do anything silly now, anything else I mean, and if there's anything you want...'

'There's nothing, Father. Thanks for coming.'

'Sorry I had to, to this place, I mean.' He kissed Sarah, ruffling her hair. 'Get better quickly.'

He turned to Peach. 'I'd like you to see my Montezumas. I've an entire bed of them and it will be like watching the sunset. Tell me how are the studies? Don't you find the Law fascinating? I have ampelopsis outside the kitchen, colour in the autumn when everything else is finished. Sarah must bring you. I forgot.' He kissed Sarah again. 'From Barnaby and I was to say how you looked.'

'How do I?'

'Fine. Enough of mischief now, attend to your books – they don't let you down.'

They watched him walk down the ward, bowing courteously to Sister at the door.

'He appears to be rambling,' Sarah said, 'it plays havoc with Counsel who imagine his attention has wandered. It's just an act. He has you neatly docketed and pigeon-holed while babbling about his Montezumas.'

'How scarifying,' Peach said. 'Wasn't he furious? How did he know you were here?'

'He went to the flat. Ronnie told him. Poor Ronnie.'

'What did he say to you?'

'He was very angry I went to the witch. I should have known better, he said. Before you came he was grumbling about the price of Eclipse.'

'What's that?'

'Fish Manure.'

'Only angry about the witch?'

'That I risked my life. I know what he's thinking, though, I always have. He never scolded even when I was a child.'

'Never?'

Sarah shook her head.

'I remember the first time. I went with a boy I mean. I was sixteen and it was summer time, very hot, there was a mist on the top of the mountains. His name was Arthur and he was in the Navy, home on leave. I thought he was very glorious. We were going swimming after tea, it's the best time with the sea very quiet and warm and the headiness of a long summer day collected up. As it turned out it was a bit too heady. We swam for a long while, then we lay on the sand among the dunes and Arthur said he loved me, although I knew quite well he didn't, it was the effect of the sun and the swim, and I said I loved him and he knew very well I didn't either, and we took off our clothes although there wasn't very much to take off, and made love. They say the first time's never any good, but whoever invented that one doesn't know what he's talking about because it was glorious and I thought I'd die of happiness there and then at sixteen on the beach at Aberllan.

'I didn't die, though, I fell asleep instead, and so did Arthur. All the exercise had been too much. When we woke up it was after ten and dark and we were very cold because we only had our swimsuits.

'We didn't say much going up to the house, it was rather a depressed feeling. There was a light on in Barnaby's room and I knew she'd gone up, and a light in the study, so I knew that Father hadn't and was waiting, so there would be no escape. I wouldn't let Arthur come in; there wasn't any point and he looked quite relieved. I got as far as the first stair when Father came out of his study.

'"Come into the kitchen," he said.

'I followed him in. There was my dressing-gown on the Aga, warming, and some milk in a pan.

"I put some whisky in it. Drink it down, girl, or you'll catch your death."

'"We went swimming," I said. It was my conscience speaking.

'"It was a long swim."

'That was all he said, just watched me drink the milk and stop shivering. I knew from his face that he knew very well where I'd been and what had happened.'

'Didn't he mind?' Peach said.

'Of course he did. He will administer the law of the country, but he will not pass judgment upon another human being outside the courts. He believes in teaching by example. I know what you're thinking. I might have led a different life if he hadn't been such a gentleman, if he'd "taken the stick to me" as they say. But you'd be wrong. It would not have made the slightest difference. He is a very respected man in Wales both in his profession and outside. And his garden is a thing of great beauty; he believes there is not sufficient of it in people's lives.'

'You take after him,' Peach said. 'You never get angry or agitated.'

'Where's the point?' Sarah said, very Welsh. 'There's none at all.'

The sun was in her eyes as she came out of the hospital.

'Darling!' A voice said.

'Henry. How did you know I was here?'

'Guessed. I have a free afternoon.'

'I haven't. This is my lunch hour. I have to go back for a Tutorial. Besides...'

He took her arm. 'Besides what?'

'Nothing. Where shall we go?'

115

They went to buy a patella hammer. There were shiny bedpans and a wheelchair in the window of the shop. They walked through the artificial limb department and up the steps into Surgical Instruments. Henry examined the hammers for size and weight while Peach looked over the sterilisers at the women in shopping hats avoiding the pavement cracks with their slim heels.

Henry showed her a hammer. 'This is a beauty.' It had a shiny wooden handle a heavy rubber wheel at one end. He handled it with affection.

'Perhaps your wife prefers the metal handle,' the black-coated assistant said. 'Would she care to see it?'

'I think this will do.'

'It's purely a matter of taste Sir. Shall I charge it?'

'If you don't mind.'

Outside Henry said: 'It's splendid. I shall enjoy using that.'

'A patella hammer!' Peach said. 'You're crazy.'

He kissed her in Wigmore Street. 'With love.'

Wife, the assistant in the shop had said. Henry's wife. A man who could go into raptures over a patella hammer. It could just as easily have been a scalpel or a Spencer Wells.

Henry took her arm. 'Three weeks today.

Do you realise? We'll go out tonight; cele-brate.'

They crossed the road. 'You spoil me,' Peach said. 'Where shall we go?'

In the Diplomat the light were shaded, a band in cerise satin shirts played South American music.

Henry was watching her. 'I like you with your hair like that.' She had wound it into a knot on top of her head. 'I like you.'

They had spent the afternoon at the Ideal Home Exhibition, tasted samples of Dutch cheeses served by girls in National Dress, instant puddings, mock-turtle soup from paper cups. They stopped by a roped-off area where children, attended by nurses, played happily. Peach watched them as dungareed they urged on rocking-horses, slid down chutes. 'Aren't they sweet?' she said. Henry was watching a child with a bandy leg.

They ordered dinner. The waiter gathered up the outsize menus, bowed and went away.

'I suppose you bring all your girls here,' Peach said.

'There's only one.'

'I meant before.'

'There was no before. I love you. I can't get on with my work.'

Peach thought of the stupid things she had done in the last two weeks: taken messages for Elliot and forgotten to give them to him, discovered at the tube station she'd come out without her purse, mistaken the time of Professor Ramsay's lecture, shopped for bread and left it on the counter.

Henry took her hand. The couple at the next table sitting in the arid silence of the middle years of marriage watched them.

'Dance?'

On the floor she closed her eyes partly conscious only of the music. When she opened them Henry was looking at a tall blonde in a white dress.

'Who's the girl?'

'You don't think...'

Peach sighed. 'You had on your working face. What's the matter with her?'

'Early Dupuytren's Contracture, look there on her hand. I could take her in and put that right in no time.'

She leaned her cheek against his as he spun her round, aware that he was still watching the girl.

'Henry darling?'

'Yes?'

'Don't you think we could take the evening off?'

Eleven

'God made everything, didn't he?' Veronica said. 'Even my teddy?'

'Yes,' Lesley said.

'And my flannel and my toothbrush?'

'Everything, yes.'

'Then who made God?' She was in the bath spreading her flannel over her thin chest like a poultice.

Kneeling on the bathmat Lesley watched the way the wet tendrils of hair curled on her neck.

'I don't know. No one. He's always been there.'

Veronica rubbed soap onto the flannel.

'It smells nice.'

'Roses,' Lesley said. 'That's why it's rose-coloured.'

'Can you get blue soap?'

'Sometimes.'

'What smells blue?'

'I don't know. It's time to get out. Pull the plug out.'

'I haven't had a swim.'

'Hurry and have it then.'

'Can I have a story?'

'If you're quick.'

'Why do I always have to be quick?'

Lesley hugged the thin body in the bath-towel. Children are so vulnerable. Like a culture plate they grow everything that falls upon them. Everything sticks.

'Give me your leg. No, the other one.'

'I wish I had orange hair like you.'

'Yours is a pretty colour. Brown, like Daddy's.'

'I wish I had a Daddy. Sonia's Daddy bought her a doll with real hair.'

'You've got lots of dolls.'

'Not with real hair.'

'You get fed up with them after five minutes.'

'I wouldn't if it had real hair.'

'Put on your pyjamas now while I tidy up.'

'I can have a story, though?'

'If you hurry.'

She went into the kitchen, stirred the soup and put plates to warm in the warming drawer.

'Who's coming?'

'Slippers! How many times have I told you.'

'Is it Auntie Eileen?'

'No, it isn't.'

'Who is it then?'

'No one you know.'

'What's her name?'

'It's not a her. Dr Gatehouse.'

'Can I stay up?'

'No, you can't.'

'Why can't I?'

'If you're not in bed before I count a hundred there'll be no story. One, two...'

'Count in your head.'

Lesley wondered if the steak was big enough. It was a long time since she had cooked for a man.

'I'm in bed!'

'Coming.' She got out the frying pan.

'How many?' Veronica sat in bed, her book open.

'How many what?' Lesley folded her school dress on the chair, took out clean underwear, socks.

'Did you count?'

'Fifty-four.'

'Will you read two stories?'

'One. What have you done to your belt?'

'We were playing horses. Michael pulled me.'

'I'll put some cellotape on it. I can't get another until Saturday.' She sat on the bed and took the book. 'Is this the one?'

'Yes.'

'Move your legs, then.'

It was hard to concentrate on the adventures of little Noddy and his interminable rhymeless songs.

She closed the book.

'Oh!'

'What is it?'

'I wanted to put my marker in.'

'I shall remember the page. Say your prayers.'

'Can I have a drink?'

'You had one just before.'

'But I'm thirsty. It wasn't a very big drink.'

'All right.'

Lesley fetched the drink, pulled the curtains and tucked Veronica in.

'Good night.' She smelled of soap and small girl; the face of innocence.

Veronica put her arms round Lesley's neck.

'You're strangling me.'

'I love you.'

'You're playing for time. No more now. Good night.'

'Good night.' She turned on her side.

'See you in the morning.'

''Morning.' Her finger was in her mouth.

Lesley shut the door gently and waited for Grant.

'Dinner ready?' Elliot said.

'Whenever you like. It's only us.'

'Those two are never at home these days. Where do they get to?'

'Peach spends every moment she has with Henry but where Grant is hiding I don't know. Whoever she is, she's lasted a long time for Grant. It would be more to the point if he found himself a job.'

'He's applied for several. He can't do

much more at the moment.'

'Funny about Peach and Henry. She used to run a mile from any medical student Grant brought home.'

'You can hardly call Henry a medical student. He's in line for the Consultantship; Professor Hopkins is getting on. He has his father's brains and his mother's looks. Fortunate it wasn't the other way round. He seems very keen on Peach. Does it make you feel old watching them play the mating game?'

'It makes me feel young. Then I look in the mirror and think "Poor Elliot, married to that".'

'I've weathered a bit myself.' Elliot patted his tummy.

'You remember Padwell?'

'Cigarettes?'

'That's right. He had a pulmonary embolism while he was in Jamaica staying with his brother. They flew him back and he's in the Middlesdon. I went to see him today and I don't fancy his chances, anyway that's not the point. You know he has this villa at Antibes. He won't be using it this summer, if he ever uses it again, poor chap. He asked me whether we'd like to go down there for a few weeks; it sounds magnificent.'

'I can't get away before the end of September. I have at least four deliveries booked for August. Besides, it's too hot.'

'I wonder if the children would like to go; take a few friends. Padwell wouldn't mind.'

'It would do them both good. I don't think Peach has any plans for the Long Vac. What about his wife?'

'Padwell's? She's in Mexico with some artist Padwell hired to paint her portrait. Not that Padwell cares; he has his own sidelines.'

'Odd lives some people lead.'

'We all end up in the same place.'

'I wonder whether we do.'

'Vino!' Grant said and put the bottle on the table. 'Grand Hermitage '54.'

Lesley measured Worcester Sauce into the frying pan. He put his arms round her and kissed the back of her neck.

'Go inside, there's a dear, this is a very delicate operation. Help yourself to some sherry.'

'I finished it on Wednesday.'

'Just go inside, then. I shan't be long.'

'You smell exotic. What is it?'

'Onions. Now go away.'

'Don't be long.'

She added lemon juice. 'I'll try not to.'

The sitting-room was tidy, the table laid for two with linen mats. The electric fire was on and Grant stood in front of it. The room had become familiar to him. In the past few weeks he had spent almost every evening in it, listening while Lesley talked, watching while she mended Veronica's clothes, helping her with the dishes. Tonight was the first time he had been formally invited. The other nights he had just knocked on the door and waited, anxiously, for his first sight of Lesley. The image he carried with him all day was invariably pale against the reality. 'I'll cook dinner for us,' Lesley had said and immediately everything was changed. Previously he had just arrived, arrangements never made for the future. A drift of comfortable evenings during which the silences had become longer, the conversation less fluent. The drift had almost ended, Grant knew; something had to break. She was a lovely girl; the loveliest person he had ever met. As well as her outward beauty there was an inward one, you saw it in her smile, her gentleness, her acceptance of a life in which she was mother and father and breadwinner.

'Right,' Lesley said. She was carrying two soup cups. Grant took one from her and put it on the table.

'Where shall I sit?' She had laid one place at the top and one at the side.

She pulled out the chair at the top of the table. 'Here.'

He kissed her.

'I hope you're hungry.'

He looked at her as she sat down. 'Starving.' The slow blush he loved embraced the freckles as she picked up her spoon.

'This is wonderful,' Grant said.

'There's a secret. You have to have eight different vegetables. It doesn't matter what they are but there must be eight. I used to love cooking.'

Like an abyss the past lay between them.

Lesley carried an oval silver platter from the kitchen.

'Steak Diane. I hope you like it.'

Grant wondered if Graham had. Opened the wine.

She served him with the steak, fried potatoes, green salad. He raised his glass. 'To you with love.'

'To you,' Lesley said.

'You've never told me about Graham.'

She looked quickly. 'I thought tonight...'

He wanted to cross the abyss. 'I don't want there to be any blanks.'

'First tell me how the steak is.'

'Fabulous.'

'If he sounds dull it's because you can't describe the third dimension, the sound of his laughter, the rapport.'

'I'll use my imagination...'

'I told you, he was doing Paediatrics at Luke's. It was his way with children that first attracted me. He didn't go all coy and baby-voiced and tickle them in the stomach or give them Smarties. He'd just stand by the bed or cot sometimes for minutes at a time saying nothing at all. It's difficult to explain but the child, even if it were crying or upset, would feel his … his calm, I suppose you'd call it, his understanding, and a link would be established, before he'd said a word. Examining them was easy. His movements were very slow, deliberate, nothing to frighten or alarm. When he'd finished he would pull up the bedclothes and tuck them in himself. Then he'd sit on the bed if the child were well enough and old enough, and talk. It used to annoy the Sisters. First of all he would crease the sheets, then he'd take twice as long with his round as he was supposed to. He'd stop and tell jokes to the older children; they were terribly long and very involved but the children loved them. There was one particular one that was a favourite with all of them.'

'Tell me,' Grant said.

'It isn't at all funny really. It's about a man who goes into a baker's shop and asks them to bake him a birthday cake, chocolate inside and white icing. They tell him it will be ready on Wednesday. On Wednesday the man goes back, inspects the cake, says yes, it's very beautiful but would they please write "Johnny" on it in blue letters. He returns the next day and there is "Johnny" written in blue. Yes, very beautiful, the man says and would they please add seven candles. He goes back again the following day and says, one final thing, he would like it decorated with silver balls and crystallised violets – Graham could expand it for hours, but I'll cut it short. He finally goes to the shop, pays for the cake and compliments them upon the decorations. Shall we wrap it up they ask him. Good gracious no, the man says, I'll eat it here, I'm Johnny.'

Grant smiled.

'I told you it wasn't terribly funny but it sent the children into hysterics. They'd repeat Graham's stories to anyone who'd listen, more often than not missing the point completely.

'Our marriage was inevitable. We were drawn to each other right from the beginning. Of course it made medicine that much more difficult for me. At one point, soon after I became pregnant I think, I almost gave up. I'm glad I didn't. We had six years, then Graham began to complain of stomach pains. When they got worse I told him he should do something about it, have some investigations, and he told me he had. Afterwards I discovered what had happened. He had breezed into the Medical Department one day and said to Saunders, who's the chief, "I've a frightful pain in my gut, old man: ask your dispenser for a bottle of something or other." Saunders wanted to have a look at him, of course, but Graham said he'd no time, give him the bottle and he'd come back if it got any worse. By the time he did go back it was too late. Jellaby did a resection of the ascending colon, which we told Graham was a division of adhesions, and after that he seemed to be fine.

'Almost a year later he got secondaries in the liver and we told him that he had infective hepatitis. He died the day before Veronica's fourth birthday.'

'He didn't know what was the matter with him?' Grant said.

Lesley shook her head. 'We had so many plans for the future. He was working on his MD thesis and we were going to build a house. We had the plans drawn up.'

'Perhaps he didn't want to know.'

'I don't think it was that. He simply never thought of illness in relation to himself. Illness was for the patients, his was just a temporary indisposition. The end was quite merciful. He became very confused, then comatose, then he was gone. They say you can't believe it. You can't. You know that you'll wake up in the morning that it will all have been a bad dream. Of course it isn't a dream at all, but a reality one simply does not care to face.'

'You're still in love with him.'

'Graham's dead. You asked me to tell you.'

'I wanted to lay the ghost.' He put down his knife and fork on the empty plate. 'Is there anything you can't do?'

'Live in the past,' Lesley said. 'I've sud-

129

denly discovered.'

She put the plates on the sideboard and put cheese, celery and biscuits onto the table.

'Help yourself. There's fruit if you'd rather.' She stood up to fetch the bowl. Grant put an arm round her waist and pulled her onto his lap. 'I'm no longer hungry; at least I am…'

She had a white neck, Leda and the swan.

'When I first came up here I promised… I want more than anything to make you happy…'

Her mouth was a hair's-breadth away from his own.

'The decision is mine,' she said.

Twelve

'Tell Henry I won't be long when he arrives,' Peach said.

'Are you listening, Grant?'

'Yes. Yes, all right.' He was thinking of Lesley. 'Did you know it was the first time for me?' he'd said when it was time for him to go. After midnight and the cheese still untouched on the table. 'You've brought me back to life,' she said. 'Everything has significance. I shall look forward to tomorrow.' 'It is tomorrow,' he said. 'The day I was born.' 'I'll bring you flowers on your birthday. Lesley, I'm just crazy about you. Do I have to go?' 'Veronica!' 'Yes, Veronica. I'm jealous of her because she's something of yours in which I have no part. Did Graham tell you you have a fabulous skin; no blemish anywhere and everything,' he put out his hands, 'everything in the right place and just enough. Like looking at the sun.' 'I'm only a woman.' 'All women.' 'Grant you're...' 'Yes? You were going to say sweet. Don't patronise, please. Please. I know you don't love me. Give it time, Lesley. I shall bombard you with love. I have an immense potential for loving you.' 'You ought to go,

Grant. I have to work tomorrow.' 'Of course, I'm being selfish.' The milk-white body, curving hips. 'I'm powerless.' She put on her dressing-gown, pulling it round her throat. 'There!' 'That's just provocative.' 'What am I to do?' 'Kiss me.' Lesley. Lesley, Lesley, Lesley. God, how did people get through the day; days of being in unbearable love.

'Why don't you bring her home?' Peach said.

'Who?'

'Whoever it is you're mooning about all the time.'

'She can't get out. She's a widow with a child.'

'We don't make it easy for ourselves. Did Dad tell you about this villa at Antibes?'

'Yes.'

'Coming?'

'If Lesley will.'

'Is that her name?'

'Yes. What about Henry?'

'I'll ask him tonight. Sarah's delighted, she's feeling pretty groggy after her do.'

'Ronnie?'

'Yes. Fleur's coming too if her holiday job doesn't materialise. It's with a paint firm. Painting house numbers on gates in America for three dollars a time. What about Clive and Berry?'

'They'll come like a shot if it's free.'

'We shall have to buy our own food. It

should be fun. When will you ask her?'

'Tonight.'

'You look as if you could do with an early one. I'm going up to change.'

'May I borrow a nail-file?' Peach said.

Hilda was brushing her hair.

'Here.'

'Thanks.'

'Where are you off to? We never see you.'

'A pub in the country Henry knows.'

'I saw Sarah today. She came for her follow-up. She needs to take things quietly for a while. I told her to tell her young man...'

'"Young man!"' Peach said. 'You're as bad as Dad with his "fast". It's all so terribly pre-war.'

'What do you know about the war?'

'What I've heard. Points, ration-books, buzz bombs, air-raid shelters, black-outs, evacuation, gas-masks, sirens, all-clears...'

'They used to dig them out from buildings,' Hilda said, holding her hairbrush in her lap. 'When they came in they were covered with debris. On the bad nights we'd work without a break until the first light. When it was over, after the last all-clear, we went to Germany. In the camps there were men who weighed no more than little children, women like walking broomsticks, broken wrecks of women with empty eyes...'

'We were scarcely born,' Peach said. 'It

wasn't our fault.'

Hilda looked at her. 'It's hard to believe an entire generation has grown up who remember nothing except what they've heard.'

Peach tried to picture her mother working among the debris of the bombed buildings and wondered whether she was wearing her navy-blue suit and if there was dust on it.

'I'm glad I was too young to remember.'

'It wasn't very pleasant, to say the least.'

'It didn't worry you though, people with their … brains blown out.'

Hilda looked at her. 'Sometimes, Peach, you say the most extraordinary things.'

'I suppose I have extraordinary thoughts. They seem extraordinary in this house, anyway.'

Hilda put away her hairbrush and looked at Peach in the mirror, the distance between them magnified. 'Tell Sarah to take her tablets,' she said, 'they're absolutely essential.'

They were in the study. Hilda and Elliot, Grant and Henry. Peach could hear them talking.

'…Sprengels deformity,' Henry was saying. 'She had a premature delivery at thirty-two weeks – it died after six hours. After that she had a hydrocephalic child with extensive spina bifida, delivered at forty-three weeks by perforation.'

'Are the parents healthy?' Hilda asked.

'Yes.' Henry's voice. 'But naturally they are apprehensive about the chances of producing a normal child.'

'Any history of congenital abnormalities in either of their families?' Elliot asked.

'None at all.' She could imagine Henry standing, sucking at his pipe, wearing his working face.

'If the Sprengels deformity in the first child was limited to the position of the scapula,' Hilda said.

Peach looked once more in the mirror. I do not exist. They never give it a rest, never.

'I suppose it would be worthwhile checking there was no spinal column malformation...' Henry said with enthusiasm.

'...also exclude any malformation in the prem.' Grant.

She stood in the doorway. Henry was as she had pictured him. God, how I love him. Grant and Elliot were standing on either side of him. Hilda sitting on the arm of the chair. They are engrossed, welded together. Where do I come in? I don't. I love one of them desperately, all of them in a way. I do not love what they love.

'...I would say about a one in twenty-five risk of a major central nervous system deformation,' Hilda said.

'And shoulder deformity?' Henry said, then looked up. 'Peach!'

'Fascinating conversation,' she said.

135

'Yes,' Henry's eyes lit up, 'I came across it last week in my Outpatients at Ealing...'

'She's kidding,' Grant said.

Henry stopped smiling. 'Of course.'

'Shall we go?'

'Don't you want a drink?' Elliot said.

I just want to get out. 'No thanks.'

'I shall be interested to hear what happens,' Hilda said. 'You're going to follow it up?'

'Of course. I'll let you know. Well, we're off. We may be late, this place is quite a long way. Don't worry about Peach.'

'I know she's in good hands,' Elliot said.

'What is Sprengels deformity?' Peach said, in the car.

'I'm not going to tell you.'

'Why?'

'You don't want to know. Do you?'

'No.'

'Why did you ask?'

'I was being polite.'

'We've started on the wrong foot. What upset you?'

'Nothing.'

'I love you. You can't lie. We were talking shop. It made you angry.'

'You belong to them.'

'To you. You know that.'

Peach shook her head.

'Don't let's argue.' Henry took her hand. 'Not tonight...'

She should have known. Perhaps she did. The evening was too perfect. The pub with its English cooking, high backed chairs, pews from an old church, air of timelessness, had been a delight; the drive back along moon-frosted lanes, an oasis of content.

She sat close to Henry; not talking; not needing to. The mutual interchange of powerful feeling. They thought the same language. With Henry there was peace as there was with no one else. Parker was all right; Parker was fun, he made you happy, but not because it was you; because he was Parker. Mother and Dad you could talk to if you didn't disturb the surface, as soon as you attempted a little depth you floundered in misunderstanding. Grant; funny about Grant, she'd got on better with him lately than she ever had, perhaps because they were both in love; they had an ear for each other's problems, half an ear, at any rate. Sarah demanded nothing from her bed-fellows, not in the way of understanding; she was sufficient unto herself; she didn't need, not like Peach needed, to love, be loved.

Henry turned the car into a side lane and parked by a ditch.

When he turned off the ignition it was quiet. Henry not moving. She knew then; wasn't sure; talked to deflect him.

'What did you think when you first saw

me? At Sarah's.'

'I thought there is the girl; the one.'

'Just like that?'

'Just like that. Tonight was good,' Henry said.

'Who told you about that place?' she said into his shoulder.

'Jason.'

'Jason?'

'He's a radiologist. He lives round there. I'd like you to meet Jason. You haven't met anyone. I've told them about you.'

He was back in the hospital, Peach could feel it, talking to Jason the radiologist, the others with their white coats, their stethescopes; back with Sister, the porters, the patients, back in his own world.

She put her face up, to get him back. When he didn't kiss her she knew.

'Peach?'

She had anticipated the question weeks ago. Relegated it to the back of her mind.

'Will you marry me?'

Marry Henry. Spend the rest of your life on the periphery of a clinical meeting. Play second fiddle to an endless succession of damaged bones. Fall in step with the jangling phone, which would summon him away for hours; hours. She knew the pattern too well. I shan't be long. Long was a purely relative term. Sorry darling it was more complicated than we thought. We had to do a … her blood pressure dropped like a bomb… But I don't want to know about the blood pressure of someone about whom I don't care two hoots. I don't want my home filled with broken scapulas or should it be scapulae I suppose it should really and greenstick fractures. I want a house that is a home with children perhaps and … Henry. Henry yes, not Henry shared with a hundred faceless names.

'I don't have to tell you what it entails.'

He was looking at her, silhouetted by the moon.

'I have to know, Peach. I can't carry on not knowing. I love you and I always will.'

She wanted to lean into the oblivion of his face.

'I need time to think.'

'You've had all your life.'

'In a little while.' She turned to him. 'Henry, please?'

'It's the end of the road, Peach; or the beginning. You choose.'

The road. Patients and patients: bed after bed after bed after bed stretching along the road as far as she could see and bending over them was Henry working along the line to eternity. The dinner was in the oven but he would never be home; never. The Ideal Homes, something inside her said, The Tate, the National, the river at Bray; the good times; Henry loving you, floating into the dark. He was working his way along the beds further and further into the distance until he was only a tiny dot in his white coat and she was running after him into the darkness and she was crying.

'Couldn't we just…'

'Drift on?' Henry said. 'I don't think you quite understand. I love you. I want you to be my wife. I couldn't really expect you to tie yourself to a life you hate, that you've been struggling to get away from. If you want to get away it would be better if you said so now.'

'Not from you.'

'It's indivisible. You know that. What's it to be, Peach?'

She felt the tears running down her face.

He gave her his handkerchief, and it was all over.

'Look, don't worry. There'll be somebody else.'

She dried her eyes. 'I don't want anybody else.'

He put the car into gear and reversed into the main road.

'Don't worry about it.' The voice was strange. She didn't know this Henry. 'It probably wouldn't have worked.'

'Probably not.' They were driving into the moon and she was afraid to touch him.

INTERLUDE

One

The cicadas filled the hot night with noise
beyond the shutters. Inside, beneath the
single sheet, Peach lay awake listening to the
mosquito which buzzed a trail around the
cornice and from time to time descended to
dive-bomb the spot where she lay. If she
didn't want to be covered with bites by
morning she knew that she should get up,
close the shutters, put on the light and
repeat her nightly gymnastics with the
Flytox spray, standing on the bed, the chair,
the table, until she had caught him. Do what
we can summer will have its flies. Emerson
wasn't it? He was usually right. It was suddenly quiet. She turned over, sweating, in an
effort to get comfortable. It wasn't so bad in
the day beneath an umbrella in the gravelled
garden, on the beach close to an inviting sea.
At night the air had weight, density. She
slept naked but even her skin was too hot.
Another turn; zoom. She pulled the sheet up
over her head quickly. She'd thought him
asleep, but he was waiting for his moment.
He circled her head a few times then the

sound died. A minor irritation in a Mediterranean summer that brought unexpected moments of content; bare feet on tiled floors; figs growing; the light-house and the little church on top of the wooded hill; opaque evenings; breath-taking mornings with air like diamond-studded cream. White sand hot on the soles; smell of panbagnat, cold touch of Ambre Solaire; ease of dressing; large cheap peaches; vin rosé; ripe Roblechamp; warm bread smell in the patisserie, cool musty one in the Epiçerie; black-clad women; swaying on the crowded raft; open-eyed in the clear water; dripping legs; rough towels; white rocks; books; sunglasses; long bright cars with burning leather; sleeping streets at midday; ro bells; no telephones; no differential diagnoses at the breakfast table with the soup-sized cups of bitter coffee, no Henry.

Henry.

He hadn't written.

The key to the letter-box hung in the hall. Peach always got it first, crossing the tiny white stones on the drive with hardened feet. The letter-box was covered with ants. Inside there were cobwebs, the odd letter for Sarah for Lesley. Nothing from Henry. The day stretched into the distance, to be endured as the others had been endured, to be lived, surface-wise like the ants. Smiling, laughing, participating with slight enthusiasm. Within, nothing.

Around her was love. Grant and Lesley, smiling faces touching limbs. Sarah, watched by a solicitous Ronnie, soaking up the sun like a lizard, regaining her strength. Clive and Berry with their jokes and succession of bikini-clad mermaids, sun-ripened peaches theirs for the picking. Fleur and Gustav, the white-haired Swiss ski-instructor she had found on the beach. The sun was hot. The *marchands de marriettes*, feet dragging in the sand, shouted '*tout chaud*' for someone else. Often in the morning she decided she would go home. By evening she realised there was no point.

'What's happened to Henry?' Hilda said, before they'd left. 'We never see him.'

'Sensible girl,' Elliot answered. 'She's busy with exams.'

Exams. Endless, endless hours at neat-rowed desks the only sounds the tick of the clock and the slow feet of the invigilator thinking of Henry. She handed in her papers. 'There's another hour!' I know. I can't do any more. Outside, the world was still surprisingly alive. People walked, talked, went about their usual business. She'd thought them all dead.

'The villa is lined up. Take care of everything; it's very good of old Padwell.'

'Is Henry going?'

'No.'

It faced the sea from behind iron gates. The steps to the terrace were veined marble. The entrance hall dark.

They had arrived at night, she and Sarah, Grant and Lesley were coming by car; Clive and Berry from Italy on Berry's motorbike; Fleur on the train, she hated to fly.

The taxi which had brought them from their airport had gone, leaving them alone in the black stillness with their cases.

'I suppose it is the right place?' Sarah said.

'The taxi-driver seemed to know it.'

'Let's go in, then.'

Peach pushed at the gate, which creaked but remained shut.

'It must be locked.'

Peach looked in her handbag for the bunch of keys given to Elliot by Mr Padwell.

'I can't see a thing.'

Sarah lit her lighter. The keyhole was rusty and the gate squeaked as it swung open.

'We'd better lock up again. I haven't come all this way to be murdered in my bed.'

They found the key to the front door.

'Shut it before you put the light on,' Sarah said, 'or you'll let in all the wild life.'

'Where *is* the light?'

They felt the walls in the pitch blackness. Sarah flicked the lighter again and they found the switch. There was a straw hat hanging on a peg with orange ribbons. The place had a shut-up smell but was clean and tidy. There were Corots on the walls, red and white tiles, polished wood, beautiful rugs. They went from room to room. The kitchen was vast. A scrubbed wooden table, shelves circling the walls with serried ranks of shining saucepans, bains-maries, funnels, pestles and mortars, great plates and vegetable dishes.

'They take their cooking seriously,' Sarah said.

From the bottom of the stairs she called: 'Anyone at home?' Her voice echoed and returned.

There were seven bedrooms, clean cotton covers on the beds.

'I think we'll share a room for tonight,' Peach said.

In the morning she opened the shutters and stood on the iron balcony drowned in the yellow sun.

There were coloured boats, postcard bright, bobbing on a breathtaking sea, not fifty yards from the window.

'Sarah, quick,' she said. 'Come and look.'

That was two weeks ago and the wonder had faded. Each day only the sun could be relied upon. There were moments when she did not think of Henry, but not many.

'You'll get over it,' Sarah said.

She tried. A green and white striped mattress on the Plage; a Picasso drawing; dancing with Clive and Berry; walking the hot pavements in shorts, baguettes for breakfast

145

beneath her arm. This is the life, she told herself. But it was not.

The mosquito zoomed threateningly near her ear. She kept quite still, willing it away. The buzzing was getting on her nerves. She flung off the sheet and went over to close the shutters. She put on the light and her dressing-gown and reached for the spray gun. He was nowhere to be seen. The wall-paper was marked from previous assaults. He was up in the corner. No, it was only a stain. She stood very still. He was on the ceiling, greyly waiting. She stood on the bed and held the spray above her head, pulling out the lever to its fullest extent. Whoosh! The oily smell irritated her nose. Whoosh! Surely he couldn't survive that. She looked round carefully but could see no more. The clock next to her bed said two o'clock but she no longer felt sleepy, only very dry.

It was dark on the landing but in the kitchen the light was on.

Clive and Berry were playing chess.

'"Lady of Spain I adore you",' Berry sang tunelessly. 'I'll have your knight.'

There was a bottle of wine on the table. Clive filled his glass.

'There was a young lady of Ealing, who hung upside down on the ceiling... Aha!' he moved a pawn.

'Is that all you're going to do?'

'From small beginnings shall come forth

… hallo, Peach. What's up?'

Peach opened the giant fridge and took out a bottle of water.

'Drink the wine, it's cheaper.'

'There was a mozzy, driving me mad.'

'Shall I come and dispose of him?'

'I've done so.'

'The lion roared,' Berry said, picking up Clive's bishop delicately, 'and brought forth a mouse.'

'I find it difficult to concentrate,' Clive said. 'There must be a mistral in the offing.'

'Mistral my foot. You're out-generalled.'

'Where did you get to this evening?' Peach said. The water was cold, refreshing.

'We went to the Casino. Clive had a theory about number nineteen.'

'What happened?'

'I was distracted,' Clive said. 'There was a blonde with her dress cut down to her navel. I was standing behind her.'

'If I'd realised, as the girl in the factory said, that for the last ten years I've been sitting on a fortune… Check!'

'I had an irresistible desire to discover how far her suntan went. Mate, dear boy.'

'And did you?'

He pushed the board away. 'Unfortunately her husband arrived. He was ten foot tall and smoking an evil-looking cigar. I never could stand the smell of cigars.'

'Ten games to six,' Berry said, putting the

men into their box.

'I find the climate vitiating. Peach, my love, you're not enjoying your holiday. I would like to make you happy.'

'I'm happy enough.'

'She misses her Professor. What happened? Did he prefer dem dry bones?'

'I don't know.'

'In other words, Berry old sport, mind your own business. Here, drink up. It's not worth keeping this little drop to collect a nasty old sediment.'

'I'll take you dancing,' Berry said. 'Swimming, anything. Name your pleasure.'

'I'll give it some thought.' She put the bottle back in the fridge next to the remains of Sarah's unsuccessful Charlotte Russe. 'Good night.'

'Want me to come and see if your mozzy has brought his brothers and sisters?'

'I can manage, thanks.'

Berry hugged her. 'Cheer up,' he said, 'or we shall have to take you in hand.'

In the morning she woke feeling exhausted. No day is commonplace... They lied. She showered, put on shorts and a shirt, still felt limp.

On the terrace Lesley was peeling a yellow peach.

'Where's Grant?'

'Gone for the rolls.'

Down among the cobwebs in the letter-box was a letter for Lesley addressed in the enormous writing of a child, the stamps on the wrong corner.

'Nothing for you?'

'Nothing.' Why should there be?

Lesley handed her the letter.

'Dear Mummy, I like staying with Gran she gives me chocolates we saw a huge aeroplane and I was scared, love from Veronica.' It filled an entire page.

'Do you miss her?'

'Enormously. It does one good to get away, though. You're apt to get too involved in a child's world; forget that you exist in your own right.'

Grant, skinny in white shorts and plimsolls, put the rolls on the table together with the *Daily Telegraph*. He bent over Lesley and kissed her.

'You smell terrible.'

'Madame gave me a slice of sausage. It was loaded.'

He pulled a paper from his pocket with three black olives.

'Also these for "la Rousse".'

Lesley laughed. 'She knows my weakness.'

'She also knows that we owe her thousands of francs.'

'Is she getting impatient?'

'She was, but I got her onto the subject of her goitre and the matter slipped her mind.'

'We shall be down to bread and bread

soon,' Lesley said. 'What on earth's the French for a goitre?'

The day passed as the others had, with sun-filled minutes.

It was midday before they got to the beach. Joseph, who owned the particular strip of plage they went to, kept their mattresses for them. He put up a big umbrella for Lesley who couldn't take the sun. He had golden hair and his muscled body was the same colour. He was always cheerful.

It was quiet, just the sea lapping, voices insulated in sunshine. Peach sat on the edge of her mattress and decided that she would go home.

'Relax, honey,' Sarah said. She was lying next to her in a brown bikini, all brown except for her finger- and toe-nails which were orange. She had worked at her sun-tan. A dip in the sea, a walk up and down, watched by lazy eyes, to dry, Ambre Solaire rubbed in attentively, full length on the mattress, first the front, then the back, or first the back and then the front, it didn't matter really. With the passing of the days the tan grew deeper, Sarah more beautiful.

'You feeling well?' Peach said.

'Fine.' She stretched languidly, orange-tipped at either end.

'Mother said I was to keep an eye on you.'

'I think it's you who needs the watchful

eye. You make me nervous.'

'Sorry.' Peach lay back, her arms beneath her head.

'Your mother is fabulous!'

'So they say.'

'No really. One has such confidence. You see her at the end of the bed, four-square, or walking up the ward in that controlled way of hers and you know that whatever happens you'll be all right.'

Peach closed her eyes.

'You hate her, don't you?' Sarah said.

'No.'

'What then?'

Peach thought. To hate there has to be love. 'You couldn't exactly call her maternal, could you?'

'Not in the accepted sense. I don't know how I would describe her.'

'Remote,' Peach said. 'They all are. It doesn't matter what you're talking about they've half their minds on something else. Dad too; unless they happen to be talking shop.'

'Henry?'

'I liked to think that Henry was different, that I had his entire attention, but often when we were out I'd catch him looking at somebody's legs or arms or necks or funny faces and I'd know he was trying to relate whatever they had to the pictures in the textbooks.'

'So?'

'So I'm fed up with sharing people with a textbook.'

'It's no worse than sharing them with a golf-course or a club or a pub or a fishing rod or a smelly old boat.'

'You may be right. I've never had the opportunity to discover.'

'Trouble with you,' Sarah said, wriggling, 'you don't know what you do want.'

She was right, of course, Peach thought. She loved the sea, the sun, and wanted to be home: she loved Henry yet could not commit herself...

Ronnie, thin in swimming trunks, sat down on the edge of Sarah's mattress and tickled her brown stomach with a straw.

Peach looked up at the sky and on the crowded beach, lay in isolation.

Two

'Come in.'

Grant opened the door of Lesley's bedroom.

'You needn't have knocked.' Her hair flamed over the pillow.

Grant, in shorts only, flung open the shutters.

'Isn't it wonderful,' Lesley said, 'to be sure what kind of day it is. I wonder if it becomes tedious after a while.'

He stood on the little balcony outside the window looking out over the bay.

'One feels obliged to soak it up,' Lesley said, 'store it away for all those grey London days. Poor Veronica. Mother says it hasn't stopped raining. When I look at the kids playing on the beach with hardly a stitch on I feel utterly mean. Grant...'

'Mm.' He didn't turn round.

'...you're not talking to me.' She sat up and clasped her knees, watching the boyish head. 'What's the matter?'

He let go of the railing and turned into the room, blinking. He put his hands into his pockets and sat on the arm of the chair, swinging one leg.

'What is it?'

'I had a letter.'

'Who from?'

'Cat's. I've got the job. Casualty Officer, under old Ingram.'

'But Grant, that's marvellous! How many people get jobs at their own hospitals?'

'I think Mother once did a D and C on Mrs Ingram.'

'It's still terrific. Why all the gloom?'

'Have you any idea what the salary is?'

'A rough one, yes.'

'Barely enough to keep one in cigarettes.'

'You could always give it up.'

'It'll be years before I'm earning anything to speak of. Years and years and years.'

'Why the sudden preoccupation with money?'

'It isn't sudden. I want to marry you.'

Lesley stopped smiling.

'Oh, I know it's ridiculous. I couldn't keep Veronica in lollipops. I think I shall chuck the whole thing and go into business.'

'What would you do?'

Grant shrugged. 'Anything. Sometimes I meet chaps I was at school with. They're married, some of them have got families, they've got cars and houses and lord knows what. Look at me...'

'I'm looking.'

'It never bothered me before. I was always a bit mystified by money talk. Used to

154

wonder what the hell people made all the fuss about.' He crossed to the bed and sat on the end of it, his hands still in his pockets. 'You're not in love with me, are you?'

'I love you, Grant. I think you're terribly fine.'

'It's not the same thing at all. If you're *in* love with someone it doesn't matter if they're the biggest scoundrels on earth. It doesn't matter.' He gathered up her hair with his hands and held it tightly back against her head. 'Being *in* love is different. If you were bald as a coot, had one green eye and one blue, and a nose like a beacon I would still love you. I suppose you're still in love with Graham.'

Lesley shook her head and Grant released her hair and put his hands back into his pockets.

'I'm just a rebound. I happened to be there as you were coming back to life.'

'It's not true.'

'It is true. You may tell yourself it's not, but it is. And if it isn't, why won't you say you'll marry me?'

'You haven't asked me.'

'Will you?'

The lids closed over the green eyes. 'I should have to think, Grant...'

He stood up and kicked the edge of the rug. 'What the hell! I haven't the money, anyway...'

'You forget I'm earning a pretty good…'

He faced her from the middle of the rug. 'I hadn't forgotten. But it's a bit of a bloody fine way to start. If you were crocked or something for a bit we'd all be on the breadline, you, me and Veronica.' He banged his forehead with his fists. 'I'm crazy about you Lesley, crazy. Sometimes I think I shall die just from loving you. When I close my eyes you're there, when I turn my head you're there, when I eat, drink, sleep, wake, walk, talk…'

'Come here,' Lesley said.

He sat on the bed again. 'And there's another thing – I'm four years younger than you.'

'So?'

'I don't know. It's just one of the things I torture myself with. I have no money; you have a child; I couldn't do enough for you both; you may want someone older…'

Lesley put out her hand. 'Come to bed.'

Grant smiled for the first time. 'It may not be a solution to the problem,' he said, 'but it's a good idea.'

'…*gelée framboise, tete d'ail, vinaigre de vin,* twenty-four *oeufs,* four *pains, cornichons, anchois, poudre néocide* … fat lot of good that's done … *sac p.d. terres, chappelure, lait, farine, pêches mures, confiture framboise, levure, alsacienne, astra, haricots verts, allumettes,* more

156

gelée framboise, tomates, tide, olives noirs, sucre
… no wonder we're all as fat as pigs. I think
that's all.' Peach laid the last scrap of squared
paper black-inked with spidery writing on
the kitchen table.

'Well, we've certainly had it all,' Sarah
said, ticking the last item. 'And I'm afraid it
comes to nine thousand six hundred and six
francs. I really think I had better go and
pay.'

'I'll go. I've nothing else to do.'

'Nor have I.'

'Where's Ronnie?'

'Gone to Monte Carlo.'

'Painting?'

'So he said. There was a girl on the beach
in a white swimsuit. When she'd been in the
water you could see through it. Ronnie
couldn't take his eyes off her.'

'Don't you mind?'

'It's a dead horse. Ronnie's very sensitive.
I think since the witch it's all been a bit of
an effort. The white swimsuit, virginity, it all
adds up in his mind. I remind him of things
sordid. It gets in the way of his painting.'

'It was his fault.'

'Darling, you don't understand. Conscience is for ordinary people. Creativity
demands an uncluttered mind.'

'Tough on you.'

Sarah shrugged. 'The way of the world.
Can you imagine Michaelangelo up on his

ceiling worrying about how many girls he'd got pregnant?'

'He was too old. Anyway I thought he didn't care for girls.'

'They say one never is. I hope they're right. If you really want to shop I'll go to the beach. We shall need something for tonight; cheap.'

'Sardines. We can fry them.'

'Fried sardines!'

'They're very good. Six-fifty a kilo. I saw them yesterday. Have we any lemons?'

'One and half.'

'That will do.' Peach took the large shopping basket out of the cupboard and collected up the bills.

'There's a letter,' Grant said, as she crossed the terrace.

'I looked in the box.'

'I got there first.' He spun it neatly into the basket.

She recognised Elliot's writing. Put on her sunglasses and opened it, avoiding the potholes in the narrow road that led towards the town. '...sorry dear to let you know you've failed. The results were out yesterday. In actual fact you only came down in one subject, the Constitutional Law. You can always take that one again, so it really could be worse. The practice is very busy, surprising for this time of the year. You remember old

Mrs Nicholson who was always so fond of you? She died last week, chronic nephritis...'

Chronic nephritis; people with their disgusting pains. She'd forgotten in the sun. She imagined Mrs Nicholson, shrivelled, she'd been old ever since she'd known her, dying, dead. The Organs of the Constitution, The Doctrine of the Separation of Powers, The Supremacy of Law. She wouldn't go back. *La Brise, Lylou, Villa Kismet,* behind gates, high walls; mattresses airing, Mediterranean fashion over balconies. *Villa Grand Mère, Mar y sol, Clopin Clopent, Gai Logis.* That was that. No Henry, no College. Everyone had something. Sarah her work, took it seriously, really saw herself in court; 'If your Worship pleases,' 'Yes, your Worship.' 'No, your Worship,' 'Objection.' 'The case for the prosecution.' Ronnie, his painting; Grant, medicine – it flowed in his veins – and Lesley. Lesley her work, Veronica. Closing her eyes she conjured up Henry, felt sick with love; God, what was the use? She couldn't live side by side with bone disease, Sprengels deformity.

From the door of the *Blanchisserie* the hot smell of steam, inside, fat women spat on flat irons, rows of sports shirts hung neatly.

The *Poissonnerie Thérèse* was crowded, she'd forgotten it was Friday. There was pushing, shouting; live fish in tanks; prices chalked illegibly on blackboards; overpowering smell of fish, pink prawns, black mussels; bosoms and elbows. *'Mademoiselle désire?'* 'Sardines.' *'Un kilo de sardines.'* They slithered bluely from Thérèse's fat fingers into the pan. How many to the kilo? Too late, they were wrapped; the swiftness of the hand. *'Six-centcinquante!'* Thérèse shrieked and was already serving the next customer. Peach pushed her way to the cash desk. *'Sixcent-cinquante,'* the cashier said. She hoped a kilo would go round. She paid the bill in the *Epicerie,* bought two melons outside the Supermarket, smelling them for ripeness, set out for home, deciding there was a certain pleasure shopping in the sun. Past the *Blanchisserie,* sheltered by palms, the road narrowed, she heard a car approaching, stood to one side. A scarlet bonnet eased by, stopped. The driver wore a white T-shirt, dark glasses.

'I recognised your tail!'

'Parker!'

'Baby!' He leaned over and opened the door.

She put the basket on the seat.

'God almighty, what's in there?'

'Sardines and melons.'

He leaned across and kissed her. 'Good to see you, Baby.'

The black sky fell into the black sea beyond the illuminated dance floor of the Casino.

You could pretend, Peach thought, her cheek against Parker's, that this was life. It was a pleasant enough pretence. The band was playing sweet music; beneath them, in a waiter-punctuated semicircle, diners sat before bloody *chateaubriands* at lamplit tables. If you shut your eyes you could blot out Henry, that there was a need to make decisions, imagine quite nicely that people, the counterfeit people, were demi-gods with no blood-sugars or atherosclerosis or raised white counts to worry about, that life was neither brutal nor short, the world a stage to be danced on.

'You still haven't told me,' she said to Parker, 'how you knew where we were.'

'Intuition,' he said into her hair.

'Seriously.'

'Henry told me.'

Peach stopped dancing. 'Henry?'

Parker nodded.

'Where did you see him?'

'At the Diplomat.'

The Diplomat.

'Who with?' Perhaps on business.

'A dame.'

'What was she like?'

'Look, could we dance? We look kind of stupid standing here.'

She followed where he led. 'Tell me from the beginning.'

'I took this Maggie dancing,' Parker said. 'I

161

was watching the dance floor while she was in the little girls' room when this dame floats by with a brown back like … like nothing I'd ever seen and a black dress, black hair all black except for that beautiful, beautiful back. Then I noticed the guy and that he looked kinda familiar and I couldn't think and it was worrying me a lawyer has to remember people. Then I remembered and I wondered what he was doing at the Diplomat with this dame. They had to pass me on the way to their table. I said hallo Henry remember? He said of course, you were waiting to take Peach to Cleo's. Where's Peach? I said and he told me, hanging on all the while to the dame with the brown back. I figured you were all washed up.'

'What did she look like?'

'I told you…'

'No…'

'Classy. Like she'd been born in a dance dress.'

'How were they dancing?'

He held her close. 'So.'

'Pretty?'

'Pretty as hell.'

Parker kissed her forehead. The saxophonist was playing a solo.

'In a week's time, Baby, you'll have forgotten Henry ever was.'

She clung to Parker to punish the girl with the brown back.

Three

She no longer wanted to go home. Home was a sun which rarely shone, a failed exam, Henry and the girl with the brown back. She saw them often, standing motionless on the dance floor of the Diplomat. Sometimes, in imagination or in dream, the girl turned round, but she was never able to see her face. Pretty, Parker said, pretty as hell. All right; she could have a good time, too. The week with Parker had passed quickly. Places needed people. He had taught her to water-ski. Concentrating on just the correct balance of the body, the stinging salt spray on face, knees, it was easy to forget. She'd followed, seeking oblivion, where Parker led; Château de Madrid for lunch, the coast from Marseilles to Menton, the Île des Porquerolles, dinner on the waterfront at Nice. Today they were going to Vence. It was a drug, taken daily, not unpleasant, a game to be played until it was time to shut the lid, return it to the cupboard. She decided on a cream shirt and skirt, noticed that her skin had tanned, imagined the girl with the brown back spending her days in Nice, Cannes, Monte Carlo. She blinked to shut

163

out the image, slid her feet into sandals, pulled back her hair in a brown headband, in the mirror saw Sarah come into the bedroom, clutching the waistband of her pants.

'Do this for me, darling.' She handed Peach a button. 'It takes me half an hour to peel them off.'

Peach threaded a needle and knelt by the window to sew the button onto Sarah's waistband.

'I'm putting on weight,' Sarah said. 'I lost it after the witch.'

'Do you ever have any regrets?'

'Never think of it.'

'Not when you see the children on the beach?'

'They have no connection with Notting Hill Gate.'

'With a little stretch of the imagination.'

'I have none. I once went out with a boy called Basil who was crazy about Brecht. He was convinced there was something lacking in my psyche. That I have no emotional depths. I can't tie myself in little knots like you do.'

'Stand still!'

'Much longer? Ronnie's waiting.'

'Two minutes. What happened to the girlfriend?'

'Gone back to Rome. We'll tag along until we get home. We're going to Pampellone. Ronnie's taking his sketch book.'

'I don't know about sketching but they hate being photographed in their birthday suits.'

'Ronnie's very discreet.'

'We're going to Vence.'

'Thank God for Parker. I don't think I could have stood another week of you doing nothing all day but rummage in that filthy old letter-box.'

'One day, Sarah-Jane, you'll fall in love and I shall laugh and laugh and laugh.'

'I told you I have no emotional depths. I'm incapable of very deep feeling.'

Peach wound the remaining cotton round the button.

'I can't decide whether you're lucky or not.'

'Card from the children.' Hilda held it up.

'The Graham girl's pregnancy test is positive,' Elliot said. 'She isn't going to be at all pleased. What do they say?'

'"Having a wonderful time."'

'Literary lot!'

'They *are* on holiday. It's a dreadful nuisance having to think of things to say. I haven't had a chance to tell you of the odd thing that happened yesterday. I don't know if you remember meeting my Pathologist at the party...?'

'Girl with red hair?'

'That's the one. Her husband died; she has

a child; terribly sad. She's away on leave just now. Anyway, I was having coffee with Florence Forsyth, she's just come back from pony-trekking – of all things at her age! – and she said I must pop up to the Path. lab and have a word with Dr Marshall about those cultures she was doing for me before I went away. I said Dr Marshall's on holiday, and Florence said, of course, how stupid of me, she's in Antibes. I said Antibes? My children are in Antibes, and she said of course, with Lesley Marshall, and I must have looked rather puzzled and she said Hilda, don't you know? The entire hospital is buzzing with it. I asked her buzzing with what? And she said Lesley Marshall and … Grant… It appears they've been having quite an affair.'

'So that's where he got to every night!'

'I must say I felt a little stupid, not having the slightest idea…'

'We'd be the last to know. The Graham girl is five minutes late and comes running, but one's children could be up to God knows what and all you get is "having a wonderful time." What Grant can be thinking of to get himself involved with a widow and child I can't imagine.'

'He's not thinking at all. They don't.'

'Perhaps it's just as well. When the time comes that you stop playing it by ear, you're old.'

'It can ruin his career.'

'He'll work it out.'
'"Having a wonderful time"!' Elliot said.

There were days one would always remember. This was one. Dropping down the steep hillside from Vence, Peach closed her eyes against the hairpin bends. A day carved like a jewel out of summer, out of life. Morning, the beginning of the idyll when the scarlet nose of the Thunderbird had climbed the winding road with the sun still fresh; dusty olive trees, terraced orchards; mirror-bright moments, as the heat grew more intense. In the villages mats were shaken out of doors, mattresses out of windows, baguettes carried on handlebars; blue-overalled workmen, the thick accents of Provençe. At home there'd be a wind, laburnum spattering the roses with golden rain, Hilda hurrying to caesars, Elliot to mumps; with the image there was no sensation of English summer breeze, of reality, only the hot embrace of the Midi. A petrol lorry labouring up the stony road impervious to Parker's horn, the driver swearing … 'fut le camp' … as they overtook it, silent prayers, aware of the sheer drop to the dry valley below. Parker's hand on her sweating one, not to worry there's plenty of room for two. Pastis in an old square, the click clack of petanque beneath the trees. In the car again, the radio on, dance music from Paris. Peace saw Henry and the girl

167

with the brown back. Her picture was never very far away. A handful of dwellings scattered on the hill; black-clad grandmothers, carpet-slippered, hated the scarlet and chrome of the thing from another world from wooden chairs outside beaded doorways.

Suddenly the Chapelle de la Rosaire, peace bedded in the uncompromising soil. A draught of spring water, the simple imprint of the artist upon the sands of time.

They had lunch at a cool restaurant set into the side of the hill. Parker found it in his Michelin. They had flaming loup with fennel, *salade niçoise,* melting cheeses from the Haute Savoie, *Blank de Blanks du Var.*

'To you, Baby,' Parker raised his glass.

'You.'

The food was good, the service impeccable. She tired not to look at the waiter's shoes.

'What's eating you, Baby?'

'It's like a rotten plum, all right if you don't bite too deep.'

'I'm not with you.'

'The waiter. Look at his shoes.'

His white coat was fresh from the laundry, trousers pressed, he lowered a dish for appraisal by two Americans in Bermuda shorts, showing gold teeth. His shoes were shabby, cracked.

'He has to bow and scrape,' Peach said,

'serve elaborate meals to spoilt tourists who leave half. At home he has a wife and ump-teen kids. There is nothing to flambé, no silver service.'

'Accept it,' Parker said. 'You can't set it to rights.'

'Will we ever?'

'The wheels are in motion. It takes time.'

'I always look at their shoes.'

Outside, the sun was high. They leaned on the stone wall of the paved garden. Far below the Mediterranean spread its silvered invitation.

'If I was a bird I'd swoop into it,' Peach said. 'The wine has gone to my head.'

Parker's arm was round her. 'We'll drive down for a dip, then I'll take you to Cannes for tea.'

The leather of the car was hot. Peach sat on her hands closing her eyes against the descent, the waiter's shoes. Down in the breathless still of midday they joined the slow crawl of sun-beaten traffic to Antibes. Overhead a silver jet came in to land at Nice.

In their own stony road a crocodile of schoolboys chattered by, magpie voices rising in the haze of heat. They flattened themselves against the wall, cat-calling and whistling as the Thunderbird eased past. They crunched to a halt on the gravel at the foot of the steps. The villa regarded them;

169

blank-eyed.

'It looks as if everyone is out,' Peach said. 'I'll get my things.' Her bedroom was cool, shuttered, the cotton cover neat, evidence of the housekeeper who had come and gone. She glanced in the mirror, brushed her hair, took a swimsuit from the cupboard.

'Parker!' Her voice echoed round the dim landing.

'Here.'

He was in his room, taking the magazine out of his camera.

'Hold this a minute for me, will you Baby? Something's getting caught somewhere.'

Peach put her things down on the bed and held the camera open.

'That's got it!'

He put the camera back into its case, wound the strap round it and laid it on the table.

'We'll take it into Cannes to be processed.'

She turned to the bed to pick up her swimsuit, her bag. Parker put a hand on her arm. 'Baby?'

'Mm?'

'C'mere.'

The afternoon lethargy and the effects of the *Blanc de Blancs du Var* welcomed his arms.

'Baby.' His eyes were closing lazily, his open mouth on hers.

The room faded. She shut out the olive

trees and the valley and the chapel on the hill, the Americans with their Bermuda shorts, the waiter's shoes and the descent towards the sequined sea. She was weightless, floating…

'Parker.' He carried her to the bed. She heard him lock the door; then he was beside her.

'Baby, Baby.' He caressed her hair.

'Parker.' She didn't recognise her own voice.

He kissed her nose, her cheeks, her mouth gently, caressing her ears.

'Baby, Baby.'

He kissed her throat, the hollow of her neck, undid the buttons of her shirt.

'Baby.'

Somewhere, someone was making love, lying with bare breasts in a Provençe afternoon.

His mouth came down on hers, he had his shirt off, brown shoulders, pressing her down onto the bed.

'Parker.'

'Oh Baby.'

He took off her shirt.

Someone, somewhere was making love.

If this was what they wrote songs about…

Length to length naked.

The ants on the letter-box, the swaying raft off Joseph's beach, the orange ribbons on the hat in the hall, Mrs Padwell's hat…

'Worth waiting for, Baby. You're beautiful. Am I beautiful, Baby?'

He was.

In the middle of the afternoon they were making love.

Breakfasts in the garden, figs from the tree, le Corbusier's 'Radiant City', the *calanques* of Cassis, the Mont Saint-Victoire, driving on the Corniche...

Someone, somewhere, love.

Eze, la Turbie, the gentle Fragonards at Grasse.

Someone.

The sun

Somewhere,

The sea

Love

Love! Do you love me, Parker? No, of course not, and I don't love you, it was only convenient and you're damned personable and know it and the sun and that enormous meal and *Blanc do Blancs du Var* and the air one hundred percent proof.

She slid off the bed.

'What is it, Baby?'

She saw her reflection in the mirror, ludicrous really, completely tanned except the breasts, a line across her back and her buttocks. She scooped up her clothes, swimsuit, handbag.

'Baby!' an animal wounded.

She turned the key in the door.

'Parker, I'm sorry.'

'Sorry!'

There was anger and disbelief on his face. She hesitated a moment, scared by his expression.

'Baby, come back – I won't hurt you.' He was pleading now.

'Parker, I can't. You don't understand.'

He sat up, his chest heaving. She thought he was going to come after her; then he collapsed onto the bed with his head in his arms.

It sounded like sobbing.

She was afraid to go into her room. She pulled on her swimsuit in the hall, then her shirt and skirt over it. She'd left her sandals in Parker's room. It didn't matter. The stairs were cold on her feet, past Mrs Padwell's hat in the hall, the cool marble of the terrace, down the white steps, running, running.

The heat embraced her.

Four

'Some sandals, please.'

'*Avec plaisir, Mademoiselle*. Of what kind?'

Gold sandals, set with gems; Judas sandals.

It was six o'clock, she didn't want to go back to the villa, face Parker, could hardly walk the streets all evening, barefoot.

'*De quelle pointure?*'

She wasn't sure; thirty something. At home it was five-and-a-half.

'*Je ne sais pas.*'

The girl sighed and went away.

She would have to go back to the villa some time, couldn't stay out all night. What did you do? Say? I'm sorry Parker. Sorry. The expression on his face; men were so vulnerable; she'd struck where it hurt most, his pride. Sorry Parker, it was the wine, the heat... You knew what Parker wanted, what he'd always wanted. Pretended this last week because of Henry and the girl; used Parker as a punchball, surprised when it sprang back...

The assistant held out some sandals. She selected a pair, not caring, and put them on.

'These will do.'

Outside the supermarket they queued for vegetables.

Perhaps if she stayed out long enough Parker would have got into his Thunderbird and driven away.

'Where's Parker?'

'Oh, he's gone,' Sarah said, 'just packed up and left.'

But of course he wouldn't have done anything of the sort. She had nothing now, nobody. Not Henry, not Parker. She would have liked to shower and change; her bathing suit felt uncomfortable beneath her clothes. When she'd run away from Parker she'd run straight into the sea. Not where the boys' school were swimming, the sea bobbing with their white caps, nor where the children played, anxious mothers calling Jean-Paul, Aristide, with their rubber rings on the water's edge. She'd run past them all to where the shore was stony, a boatman sat on a rock mending a net, jumped into the water. You could see to the bottom; small fishes darting in and out of the stones; floating, the sun scorched your face. She had taken the day and ruined it. She'd swum till she was tired. Too tired almost to walk back to the shore, the water heavy on her legs. She lay down on a rock to dry. The sun, the sea, the songs they sang, they all conspired to trap the unwary with the illusion that love could be plucked from trees when it was something you had to work out for yourself. 'Let's Make Love', 'Let Yourself Go', 'And in Lapland even Laps do it, let's do it, Let's fall in Love'. Like let's go to Fortnum's for tea and of course it wasn't like that at all. You never made a decision it just hit you below the belt; Henry at Sarah's, when you weren't expecting it. Making love was something else again, the expression were so euphemistic, sleep with, go to bed with, when it had nothing to do with sleep and not necessarily anything to do with beds or love. Men were more easily rousable Sarah said and once their passions were aroused it was difficult for them to ... what had she done to Parker? Poor Parker, she should have stopped before it had gone so far. She played the scene back.

'Baby.' Parker's hand was on her arm.

'Mm?'

'C'mere.'

She was in his arms kissing him. 'Come on Parker how about that swim?'

'Let's stay here, Baby.'

'No.'

She ran down the stairs past Mrs Padwell's hat and into the sun. Parker followed. They swam, drove to Cannes for tea...

The rock was digging into her back. She turned over and lay on her stomach. Everything was as it had been, the boatman still mending his net. When she was nine, perhaps ten, they'd gone to Cornwall for a holiday. There was a village shop, a sweetshop. The bell rang as she opened the door. Inside it was quiet, no one about. Mrs Pennyquick lived upstairs. There had been Mars bars on the counter, Fry's Chocolate Cream, there was money in Peach's purse, but that wasn't the point, she heard Mrs Pennyquick's foot on the stair, slipped a Mars bar into her pocket... 'Yes dear?' Mrs Pennyquick said. 'A Mars please,' Peach held out her money. She had a bad moment as Mrs Pennyquick took a bar from the counter with arthritic fingers; did she know how many there should have been? Would she accuse the child waiting in the shop? Send for the police? 'Better day today,' Mrs Pennyquick had said. 'Yes. Good afternoon.' 'Good afternoon.' She had expected the chocolate she had stolen to choke her, taste bad. It didn't. There was no punishment, no retribution, only a wish that it hadn't happened, that she could put back the clock. You couldn't. Parker's face. She would never forget Parker's face.

She fell asleep dreaming of Henry. When she woke the sun was low in the sky, the boatman gone. Everything ached. She wondered if she had sunstroke. The sea slapped against the rocks. She dressed, feeling out on a limb, unwanted. Walked slowly over the warm pavements towards the town where the sandals were hanging in clusters outside the shop next to the supermarket.

The sandals were uncomfortable, had a thong between the toes; retribution.

Thirsty, she sat at a pavement café, ordered coffee. Nearby a group of youths laughed over Pernods. She tried not to look at the waiter's shoes. The coffee filtered slowly. The waiter hurried, bringing drinks, mopping tables. Why couldn't she manage things better, like Sarah, Lesley, not get so involved or getting involved, not care. Two girls joined the youths with the Pernods; they had three-inch heels, hair down their backs, laughing invitingly. She wanted to warn them. It was still only half-past six. At the other side of the square a coloured poster outside the cinema advertised *'Mefiez-vous des Flics'*. High booted, tattered shirts and a pointed gun. Perhaps afterwards she would feel more composed. The laughing girls were well dug in, holding admiring designing eyes *'...and in Lapland even Laps do it...'* It was no concern of hers.

'What's your lucky number?' Grant said.

'Five.'

'Five it is, then.'

'Les jeuz son faits. Rrrrien ne va plus.' The croupier's face was deadpan, eyes ash shadowed. Lesley's head was against Grant's shoulder, red on grey, burnished copper on slate. He put an arm round her. She looked

up, smiling.

'Happy?'

'Yes.'

It wasn't enough. He wanted to hold her, put her in chains. She hadn't said any more about marrying but he'd never let her go. He tightened his hold on her. Never let you go.

'*Numero cinq.*'

Unlucky in love?

Lesley picked up the chips.

'Shall we go?'

'Women!'

'Why? Don't you want to?'

'I have a winning streak. I can double that up.'

'Buy me a drink instead.'

Grant looked at the table on which chips were raining.

'I fancy five again.'

'*Les jeuz sont faits.*'

It was too late.

'*Numero seize, noir impair…*'

Sixteen.

Cigar smoke hung low over the tables. Suntans peeled. Faces kept faith with hands.

'Bonsoir Docteur,' the dinner-jacketed watch-dog, a thousand faces stored neatly in his head, bowed from the waist, held open the glass door.

Outside, the streets were brightly lit, loud with jazz. Strollers in light clothes walked slowly, overflowing into the roadway. They shuffled along behind two youths in leather shorts; street vendors sold pancakes sprinkled with Grand Marnier, offered shots at moving bears. A Giulietta ground to a halt, police blew peremptory whistles, demanded *'papiers'*. The shops were open, inviting.

'I'd like to buy you something.'

They were passing a toy shop in which animated penguins banged drums or knitted, babies drank milk from bottles.

'Look Grant, for Veronica.'

'Not for Veronica. For you.'

'It's so long since I bought anything for myself.'

'It's time we did just that thing.' He looked in the windows. 'Perfume, a scarf?'

'One gets out of the way of it. Used to thinking in terms of steel-wool or butter.'

'I wish I was a millionaire. You'd forget that steel-wool or butter ever existed.'

Lesley smiled, the light from the shops illuminating her face.

'I didn't mean I was unhappy, one can live without scarves, perfume…'

Two girls with long pink fingernails and skirts like bells cooed into the exotic window of the *Parfumerie*. They faded against Lesley in her plain linen dress.

'God, I love you,' Grant said. 'There's a shop on the corner. I'll buy you a book.'

They had to elbow their way in. Some

English boys in grey flannels and Aertex shirts were snickering as they browsed.

'Here,' Grant said. 'Over here.'

He bought her the poetry of the Brownings because he was in love. In the shop next door Lesley bought him a red leather lighter because he could never find his matches. They walked along by the sea where the crowds were thinner.

'It's like a birthday,' Lesley said, holding her book. 'Or Christmas.'

'Not that but I have the feeling we must hold on to tonight.'

'There's nothing special,' Lesley said. 'We have another week.'

A cloud no bigger than a man's hand; the super supersensitivity of love.

'Let's sit here,' Lesley said.

They drank Cinzano.

'Give me the book,' Grant said. 'I'll write in it.'

He opened the fly-leaf. Could think of nothing to say. Darling Lesley I love you more than anything in the world? It got tatty in transposition from heart to paper. They were ordinary words, available to anyone to abuse, to distort. He opened the book at the Sonnets from the Portuguese and underlined 'How do I love three?...'

'I like watching the people,' Lesley said. 'Trying to sort out the nationalities. Germans, French, the Americans you spot a mile away…'

'I noticed no one but you.'

She looked at him. 'I don't deserve it.' She traced a pattern on the table with her fingertips. 'When I'm back among the white cells and the haemolytic steps, I shall think of this. I never thought I could be happy again.'

Grant stopped her hand with his. 'You'll never be sad again, Lesley. If it takes me a lifetime I shall see that you'll never be sad.'

Antibes retired early. Slowly, exhausted, watching the reflection of the lights in the black water, Peach walked along the deserted sea road towards the *Avenue de la Reine*. The film, which she had only partly understood, had been about a gang of dope pedlars whose nerveless chief was a girl in a raincoat and beret. There had been a great deal of shooting with surprised victims spread-eagling on the ground after final close-ups of faces grotesque with terror. Spilled out, with the local adolescents, into the empty square, she was more than ready for the villa. With any luck Parker would have gone to bed. The thong of the sandal was rubbing her toe. She had pains in her abdomen and she realised she'd had nothing to eat except a chocolate 'Eskimo' in the cinema since the 'loup with fennel' for lunch, which seemed light years away somewhere in memory, on canvas, the Mediterranean colours painted bright.

A car with headlights full on turned the corner of the Coast Road ahead, seemed to be driving slowly, hugging the kerb. She remembered it was midnight, cars often toured the roads looking for girls. There was no one about. Sea on one side, the wide road on the other. She hadn't passed anyone, either. The villas were on the edge of the town, all now tightly shuttered. The lights grew larger. She tightened her grip on her handbag thinking if necessary a good swing with that, not that there was much in it. What a stupid thing to do, hadn't thought really, could have taken a taxi from the square. It was slowing down. Foolish; the car was open, a man alone; she jumped down onto the beach, started to run, stumbling along the stones.

'Baby!' a voice called. 'Hi! Baby, come back!'

'I was scared,' Peach said. 'I thought someone was trying to pick me up.'

'They were too, Baby,' Parker said, slamming the car door. He walked round to his own side, slid into the seat, shut his door and put his foot on the accelerator. The car jerked forward.

'I really was scared.'

They were going fast down the Coast

Road in the direction from which Peach had just come; too fast.

'Where are you going?' Peach said. 'You could have turned in the road there.'

'To Monte; Monte Carlo,' Parker said. 'The night is young.'

The speedometer needle wavered at ninety.

It was then that she realised Parker was drunk.

Five

'Don't lock up,' Sarah said. 'Parker and Peach aren't in.'

'I'll leave the front door,' Ronnie said. 'Where did they go?'

'To Vence. That was this morning. They must be having quite a time.' She sat at the kitchen table turning the pages of Ronnie's sketch-book; pencil drawings, economical of line; Joseph's beach, a young man with a straw trilby over his eyes, St Christopher round his neck, sat on the edge of a mattress, chin in cupped hands; a girl in an unboned swimsuit pinned up her hair; Madame Joseph, hands on hips, as round as she was long; two feet on the water's edge; a naked child; the villa with its palms; grapes; pomegranates on a stall; small boats; cynical Provençal in a black beret; mangy cat; washing hung across a street; bougainvillea on a wall; earthenware jars with geraniums; sailors at Cannes; herself with a cigarette at Pampellone.

'These are good.'

'The only good thing about me.'

'You artists!'

He sat at the table and tore Sarah's

portrait out of the book. He slid it across. 'You can have this.'

'Parting gift?'

'I gave you something else. You didn't want it.'

'Did *you?*'

'Yes.'

'Ronnie!'

'I want to explain why I let you down. Let Peach go with you to the witch. I should have gone. I said I was going to school. I didn't. You know what I did? I sat in the park and watched the children. There were new-born ones, like little monkeys, swaddled in blankets; some with golden curls sitting up, playing with rattles; toddlers in dungarees, older ones with boats. I watched them while mine was being murdered.'

'You suggested the witch, or Skipper did, remember?'

'It wasn't for the child I minded. It was for myself. I created it as I created the boy with the hat, these pomegranates here. I'd feel the same if you tore them up; physical pain. I watched them all day. The morning ones went and the afternoon ones came. After a while they went home, too, for tea. I hung around waiting for the pubs to open. I wanted to be blind and deaf so that I wouldn't see the face crumpling, the paper tearing. Wanted to pretend it hadn't happened though I wanted it destroyed.'

'It hurt you more than me.' Sarah stubbed out her cigarette.

'I only wanted to point out that if these sketches are good it's because they have to be. I never will be. I'll never face up to anything, do anything.' He smacked the cartridge paper. 'It's all here, Sal, all of it. You know bloody well I'm good for nothing else.'

'We had a good time,' Sarah said.

'Any fool can have a good time. You don't need brains, wits, integrity.'

'Will you send me an invitation to your private viewing? Or will I be forgotten in the backlog of three thousand five hundred and sixty-five odd girls?'

'I won't forget you, Sal. You've helped me. There's one thing about being an artist. Everything you do, everything you see, everything, is of importance. It all adds up you see.'

'Glad to have been of use.' Sarah yawned.

'You have a lovely chin.' He took a pencil from his pocket and opened the sketchbook.'

'Ronnie, it's after midnight.'

He half-closed his eyes, drawing quickly. 'Girl in a Provençal kitchen.'

By day you could see Cap Ferrat, Beaulieu sur Mer, the unbelievable plunging view towards the sea.

Peach sat in taut silence watching the

187

speedometer, exhausted from pleading, cajoling, repeating: 'Parker, please!'

They were on the Corniche; once somewhere here, a village not solidly anchored had slid from its moorings down into the sea. She didn't dare to look but to the right, she knew lay the same sea, black now, that had sparkled so invitingly at midday. Black too were the shadowed palms and the road ahead except for the occasional approach of lights, a signal for Parker to accelerate, swerve until Peach swore the wheels were over the edge of the road, hoot deliriously with triumph. The road sounded wet beneath the wheels although there had been no rain; like black ribbon the Thunderbird gobbled it up, the bends disappearing beneath protesting tyres. She held tightly to the door on one side, the arm-rest on the other. Praying sometimes, trying not to think; odd thoughts, 'Listen my children and you will hear of the midnight ride of Paul Revere': don't they have police cars; doesn't anyone care? She'd never seen Parker drunk; it was frightening: Dr Jekyll and Mr Hyde, his mouth was in a straight line, hunched over the wheel, imagined he was at Silverstone. Another bend. She closed her eyes, was flung against the door. Straight now, the needle passed the hundred. Try to think of something else. They were climbing still, must be nearing La Turbie, there was a car

188

ahead, must slow down, she buried her head waiting for the crash, they were past it, swaying perilously.

Parker drunk; never seen him anything but easy-going affable, peeved sometimes, when he'd gone to find a Maggie, nothing else thought, no indication of the devil that was in him now. Perhaps if she talked...

'I went to the pictures,' she said.

'Uh?'

'The movies. About a gang of dope peddlers. They spoke *patois* most of the time, it was hard to understand.'

Silence. He took a bend, hands chasing each other round the wheel.

She took a deep breath.

'Parker, I'm sorry about this afternoon. Please don't be angry. It would be better if you stuck to Maggies.'

He turned his head to look at her. She watched the road, terrified, sorry she'd spoken, distracted his attention.

'Not to worry Baby, not to worry.'

She grabbed the wheel and straightened the car.

'Parker, the road!'

He looked ahead again.

'Definitely not to worry.'

A sign flashed by. She tried to see how many kilometers to Monte Carlo but they were going too fast. She felt sick from hunger and fright. Cold too, had only her thin blouse and the wind nearly blowing her head off. She opened the glove compartment to see if perhaps she had left a scarf. A bottle of Scotch rolled out.

'Gimme a drink!'

'Parker no!' She shut the compartment.

He leaned over to open it forgetting to watch the road again.

'All right, I'll do it.'

She took out the cork and handed him the bottle. He flung his head back and took a long drink. They were approaching a bend.

'For God's sake, Parker!'

He handed her the bottle and pulled the car round just in time. She slung the bottle into the trees.'

'What you do that for?'

'It was empty.' She was a bad liar.

'You threw away my liquor.' He sounded petulant. 'Naughty Baby threw away my liquor. Why d'you throw any my liquor?'

'I thought it was empty.'

'I'm thirsty. I had a tough day. Took a girl for a drive, no Maggie, mind, a lady. This was some lady. Had lunch in the mountains. Flaming fish. Hear that, flaming fish. Vino too, she didn't mind taking a little drink, *Blanc de blanc de blanc de...?* Something. The waiter was a little down at heel, so this lady, she was a real lady, got sore at humanity for letting this waiter get down at heel, she loved people see.'

The palms flicked by in moonlit silence.

'When we were through eating the lady says how about a swim, it was hot even in the mountains, so we go back, so, so,' he zig-zagged a hand, indicating the mountain road, 'so and so.'

They'd drifted to the left of the road. An oncoming car flashed headlights, hooted angrily, snaked past with two wheels up the hillside.

'We go back for our gear. No one at home. I want to make love to the lady, the lady wants to make love to me. You're beautiful, I say...'

'Parker!'

'...you're beautiful too she says. I go for her in a big way. She makes me feel good see, good. Then you know what she does, this lady?'

Peach shut her eyes.

'I said you know what she does?'

'Yes, I know what she does.'

'She leaves. Ups and goes. She loves people see, only not when they come too close. Like ducks. She'll throw the bread into the water.'

'I said I was sorry.'

'Sure, this was a lady. A real great lady.'

Keep him talking. He was driving more slowly now.

'Went to find me a Maggie, Juan, Cannes...'

But they didn't have a Maggie not anywhere there.

'…but they didn't look too good; not after
this lady. So I bummed around the waterfront and there was this ship, a Yankee, and
a coupla matelots wanted to see the town.
So I showed them the town.'

Drink by drink.

'Had to be on board by midnight. So I
went to find my lady. I wanted to tell her;
wanted to tell her … wanted to tell her…'

'Yes?'

'We have a word for girls like her back
home.'

Peach waited, not moving.

Parker put his foot on the accelerator. 'I
couldn't tell her. She's too much of a lady,'
he yelled.

The engine roared. They passed a white
English Consul. Peach turned back and
signalled to the driver, hoping he would do
something. Delighted, the driver waved
back and was lost in the zig-zag of the road.

They were making the descent. By day you
got your first glimpse of Monte Carlo.
Braced as for the Big Dipper, she'd always
hated the Big Dipper, Peach tried to think of
Monte Carlo, quiet Monte, streets lined with
palms, horse-drawn carriages for tourists,
white plaster villas with bright roofs…

'Parker, please!' She was near tears, hys-
teria, from hunger, fright, tiredness.

A bend; only just. He leaned over sideways like a racetrack driver. 'Nooooot to worry!' Delighted like a schoolboy. Really happy now, hands high on wheel.

The sea was black below. The next bend not fifty yards away.

Waiting for him to brake, she felt him accelerate.

'Parker, slow down!'

He was crazy now.'

'Definitely not to worry!'

They went at the bend like a shot from a cannon, into the corner which was too tight and the tyres screaming and Parker pulling the wheel round like a maniac and nothing happening. They were through the low wall and falling over and over...

It must have been a bush that held her because she remembered it like a thousand swords and she saw the car like a match when you held it upside down, the flame illuminating the hillside and not far away on his face still, like a black log, was Parker: and last of all she remembered hearing shouts a million miles away and thinking Parker please don't be dead.

Six

They were dancing; Henry and the girl with the brown back. Round and round in space quite far away but with each revolution coming nearer, spinning like a top to crashing cymbals whose sound grew louder with each turn of the couple, Henry smiling, the girl with her quick neat feet; they were life-size, then larger, gigantic, grotesque, the cymbals split her brain with their sound. Peach opened her eyes.

'Peach,' Sarah said, 'are you awake?'

The room was white; everything; curtains, walls, bed. A very shallow bed, you lie on top of it, not in it, cradled. There was a mirror opposite. In it she saw the crucifix above her head.

'There was an accident,' Sarah said. 'You and Parker. You were lucky, nothing but a few bumps; they gave you something to make you sleep. We had quite a fright, the *gendarmerie* hammering on the doors at three o'clock in the morning. You're in the Hospital. The Sisters are terribly kind. It's six o'clock. You've slept like a baby all day. I expect you're feeling hungry.'

Baby. Parker.

'Parker?' Her mouth was dry. Like a log; quite still.

'Parker's alright. You were fortunate it was an open car and that you were flung clear.'

'Not hurt?'

'Stitches in his head.' Sarah looked at the ceiling.

Sixth sense. 'Only his head?'

'Something about his knee,' Sarah said. 'They aren't sure. You were luckier.'

'He'll be alright, though?'

'Sure. Grant's got a bed at the South-West London for him. They're going to fly him back as soon as he can be moved. Apparently it's the best place for bones.'

'Professor Hopkins. Doesn't sound very all right.'

'Just that Grant thinks he'd be better at home.'

'Can I see him?'

'They're doping him for the pain.'

'It was my fault.'

'They said Parker had been drinking.'

'He wanted to make love to me. I led him on then ... walked out.'

'Didn't your mother tell you anything?'

'I don't manage things as well as you. Parker was crazy. He drove like a madman along those winding roads. I told him we'd go over the top, I told him. It was like a match.'

'What was?'

'The car. When you hold it upside down. He kept saying not to worry, not to worry, there was a bottle in the glove compartment, whisky, he said...'

'I should just rest,' Sarah said.

'...I wanted a scarf, I didn't realise the bottle was there.' She sat up, looking at her white face in the mirror.

'I couldn't stop him, you see, he just went faster and faster, I kept telling him there'd be an accident...'

Sarah held her hand and with her other pressed the bell on the locker. 'Look, you mustn't get excited.'

'...drove on and on not even slowing for the bends. I tried to wave to a car and you know what he did?'

'Peach, you must lie down.'

'...he waved back! Like an idiot, a bloody idiot; he could see we were going much too fast. I never have liked driving fast. There was a sheer drop you see...' She waved her arms.

A Sister of Mercy with a faint moustache on her upper lip glided into the room. She cradled Peach in her arms and laid her back on the pillow.

'...not to worry, he kept saying not to worry...'

The Sister stroked her forehead. *'Vous allez dormir.'*

Peach closed her eyes.

'*Elle a reçu un grand choc*. It is the shock,' the Sister said.

They were packing. Like opened champagne the holiday had gone flat, the villa turned sour on them. '*Lou soulee me fair canta.*' The motor of the poets of Provençe. The sun no longer made them sing. Slowly, each muscle an aching thing, Peach collected books from the terrace, sun-glasses and midge cream from the china cupboard, swimsuits from the balcony, flippers and goggles from the garage.

'Can't one of the girls do that?' Grant said.

She tried to fit everything into the case.

'I prefer to be busy.'

'I was packing Parker's things. I found these.' He held up the sandals she had left in Parker's room.

'Throw them away.'

'They look perfectly good to me.' He laid them on top of the case.

Peach picked them up. 'I don't want them. Put them in the dustbin.' She sat down on the bed, tired suddenly. 'You're worried about his leg, aren't you?'

Grant swung the sandals. 'He has quite extensive bone injuries. He should be all right, though. I've got him a bed at the South-West London.'

'Sarah told me. Professor Hopkins.'

'Professor Hopkins is in America. Henry

will be looking after him.'

'Henry?'

'He's the Senior Registrar, isn't he?'

The Henry that belonged to Jason, the hospital.

'Can I see Parker?'

'Better not. We want to keep him quiet till he gets home. He's very shocked. You don't like hospitals anyway.'

'It was my fault. Did Sarah tell you?'

'She didn't, no, but Parker was tight as a tick and to drive along the Corniche in that condition is asking for trouble. I don't mind him risking his own neck if he wants to be such a damned fool, but to take you with him...'

'It's not your business.'

'It is my business. You're my sister and Parker has no sense of responsibility. Bumming around, that's all he thinks of, girls...'

'You sound like Dad.'

'What if I do? I still can't see that it's terribly clever to drive like a lunatic, drunk at night...'

'Do you think before everything you do?'

He thought of Lesley.

'Look, Peach I don't want to fight with you. You aren't feeling up to much. I just want you to see this thing in the right perspective. It's ridiculous for you to take the blame.'

He held out the sandals. 'You're sure

about these?'

Peach turned her back. Like gloves, roses, stockings, all through history they opened the flood-gates of memory.

She sat near the window of the aircraft and read idly the instructions how to don her *Zwenvesten, Corsets de Sauvetage, Cintura di Salvataggio,* Life Vests, *Salvavidas* or *Schwimmwesten.* In the event she thought perhaps she wouldn't trouble. It would be quite a relief to sink beneath the cool water, not to have to think, to sort anything out anymore, to bother. They had flown Parker to England the previous day. Grant and Lesley had gone with him. Clive and Berry had gone off on the bike, Fleur by train. Ronnie was going home by way of Rome, she and Sarah had been left to lock the villa. There had been no pleasure any more in the tiled floors, the view of the bay from the balconies, the paintings on the walls. They'd closed the shutters as if somebody had died instead of just the holiday spirit; shut the door for the last time on Mrs Padwell's hat.

The flight had been delayed. In the airport lounge she'd sat languidly watching the crush at the duty-free shop; perfume, Limoges china, silk shirts, ties, people; the patient behind *France-Soir, New York Herald Tribune, The Times;* those hating the delay prowling, impotent, picking up baggage, putting it down, referring tirelessly to wrist-watches.

She'd sat patiently, remote, walking with Sarah to the tarmac, when she was told, indifferent to the fact that they were safely airborne, unmoved by the Captain's speech to welcome them aboard. Dinner on horrid plastic trays had been served and cleared away; passengers smoked, walked, talked, adjusted the air-conditioning.

'Look, he'll be all right,' Sarah said.

Peach turned away from the Alps spun with snow.

'I made a mistake about Parker, thought he had no feelings...'

'We all have.'

'...didn't care. I just trampled all over him, because of Henry.'

'Honey, Parker has no illusions...'

'I think you're wrong...'

'You must stop brooding.'

'Damn it Sarah, he may never walk.'

'Who told you?'

'It's pretty obvious.'

'Professor Hopkins...'

'He's in America.' She saw Parker on crutches instead of water skis...

'I never told you about Pampellone,' Sarah said.

'Anna Marie will bring you something on a tray,' Hilda said.

'Look Mother, don't fuss. I'm perfectly fit

except for the odd bruise.'

'How did it happen?'

'I told you. The road is very tricky there, narrow; we just went off the edge.'

'Parker must have been driving much too fast.'

'I suppose he was a little.'

'What happened to Henry?'

'In what way?'

'He didn't go with you. I suppose he was working.'

'You're out of date.'

'I like Henry. We both do. But then Ian's such a nice person.'

'There's only one thing the matter with Henry.'

Hilda sat on the bed and raised an eyebrow.

'He's in the wrong profession.'

'I thought he was terribly keen.'

'He's keen all right. I'm not, though.'

'Is that why you've stopped seeing him?'

'He wanted to marry me.'

'I'd be terribly pleased.'

'Of course you would. Out of the frying pan in to the fire. One more for your little côterie.'

'Don't you think you're being a little silly over this? People are ill, Peach, sick, we're trained to treat them, Elliot, I, Grant, Henry. It's not such a bad thing to be doing in the world.'

'If it has to go on I don't want it going on under my nose. If Mrs Smith has water on the knee I'm sorry for her but I don't want to know about it.'

'Henry isn't even in General Practice.'

'It's not like being an accountant or a solicitor. They're only too pleased to leave their books in the office. Mention a boil or a bunion to a doctor in the evening and see his eyes light up. It's not his work you see, a separate entity. It's him; it has to be.'

'But Peach, even if it is, what's wrong with being interested in your work? Sure it's better than spending your days doing something you hate?'

Peach sighed. 'There's nothing wrong for you, Grant, Dad, Henry. You care, you see. I don't. I don't want to know. I've had eighteen years of knowing every time some wretched child comes out in a rash, some fretful old man needs an enema.'

'It's nothing. These things have to be done.'

'I know they do but, Mother, I don't want to know. Can't you understand? And I don't want to be the sort of wife who says to her husband "Had a good day?" and get the answer, "yes, dear." I want to know; it'll be my husband, part of me; but not if the answer's going to be "First class. Two fractures, a dislocated shoulder and a hammer toe."'

'You love Henry?'

'Yes.'

'Then I don't understand.'

'I don't understand,' Hilda said.

They were in bed, the moon shining three-quarters full through the open curtains.

'You can't hope to,' Elliot said, turning over comfortably. 'If there was understanding between the generations there'd be no incentive to rebellion, creation, achievement. We aren't intended to understand. I suggest you let them work it out for themselves and try to get some sleep.'

Understanding between the generations.

Hilda thought of her mother. Her parents had been what was in those days known as comfortable, Hilda the only daughter for whom they had great plans. They had lived in a three-storeyed house, which today would immediately be converted into flats. The drawing-room in which she remembered aspidistras and a pouffe was on the first floor; the maids trailed up to it with brass buckets of coal. She'd worn a sailor collar, black stockings, long skirt and her hair in ringlets. 'We're giving a dance for you, Hilda. Your father's business associates. Perhaps you will meet a nice, comfortable young man.' She didn't want to dance, was gauche, awkward, despite the money they poured into Miss Drake's Academy on her behalf; certainly didn't want to meet a nice comfortable young man. There was only one thing she wanted to do passionately, absorbingly, only she wanted to become a doctor, a surgeon. They laughed at her. They gave the dance. The house she remembered had been filled with hydrangeas, masses and masses of them, waitresses came and with them mountains of food. There were young men and music, girls in light dresses, and champagne. When they looked for her to cut her birthday cake she was in the basement, her dress bloody, tending a cat that had been run over by a passing car.

'We thought a nice finishing school in Switzerland, Hilda. Herr Bondi from Zurich knows a very good one…' As if it were yesterday she saw her mother, straight-backed, uncompromising, housekeeper par excellence, bending her head over her needlework, saw herself on the footstool fiddling with the antimacassar on the chair, bursting with rage, the passion mounting inside her until she had exploded: "You don't understand! You don't *want* to understand!" "Hilda go to your room!" She had gone to her room. Was there no way she could get inside the head, the hair drawn into a neat bun, no way she could transfer just a little of what made her tick into the brain of her mother. Today of course children were allowed to have their say, but the rift remained. She had got her way at last having dramatically threatened suicide, which she hadn't the slightest intention of carrying out, to do so. Her studies were done in the privacy of her room. Her parents made it clear to her that she was a freak, a disappointment. They both died before the Second World War could upset any more of their out-dated illusions. The wheel had come full circle and she was no more able to understand Peach's unreasoned hatred for her own world than her mother had been to view with sympathy her all-consuming passion.

'Do go to sleep,' Elliot said. 'They're perfectly capable of sorting out their own problems.'

'We've rather left them to do that. Perhaps we should have...'

'There's comes a time when every parent feels he's gone wrong and runs his finger along the line to see where he's failed. He hasn't failed. It's just that the bird has left the nest, wet behind the ears and is floundering a little. There's nothing you can do except pick him up if he comes a complete cropper and put him on his feet again.'

'They're both floundering just now.'

The telephone by the bed rang loudly.

'It's Mrs Strangeways' second staging,' Elliot said, 'that will give you something else to think about.'

PART TWO

One

Grant, in Lesley's sitting-room, looked up at the sound of the key in the door.

She was wearing a raincoat, took it off as she came in, and put it over the arm of the chair.

He looked at the white neck, the long slim fingers spreading into the red hair to tidy it. How I love this woman.

'You said three!'

She looked at him quickly. He hadn't meant to reprove, had grown nervous waiting, imagining illness, street accidents.

'Sorry. Dr Bader wanted some of the back-log cleared up. There was some stuff I just had to go through myself.'

'What's the matter?'

She looked surprised. 'Nothing. Why?'

'You're so far away.' He held out his arms to pull her onto his lap. She kissed the top of his head.

'Something is the matter.'

'Just tired. First day back.' She sat on the sofa.

'Of course. I'll make you some tea. Don't

207

move a muscle.'

'I had some at the hospital.'

She kicked off her shoes and curled her feet under her. She did that the first day, Grant thought.

'How's Parker?' Lesley said. 'What did Henry say?'

'Open compound fracture of the tib. and fib. into the knee joint. He's not committing himself at the moment. I saw the X-Rays, they were a pretty horrid mess.'

'Does that mean...?'

'We shall just have to wait.' He moved to the sofa, sitting by Lesley's legs. 'We had a good time didn't we, in France?'

'The best.' She looked at him with the green eyes, tired. 'I have so much to be grateful to you for.'

'Don't say that.'

'Why not?'

'It's not the sort of thing you say to someone you love.' He took her hand. 'I wish you didn't have to be tired.'

'Just the first day. I've grown lazy.'

'Where's Veronica?'

'Out to tea.'

'Seems funny after France.'

'What?'

'The weather. Everything. Can you fix a sitter for tomorrow? I've tickets for the Royal Court. Grateful patient of Dad's.'

'Not tomorrow, Grant. We've a clinical

meeting. I really have to go. You don't mind? Just one night. A pity it had to be tomorrow.'

'I mind; yes. Not about the play though. The heroine is buried up to her neck in a grass mound for three acts.'

Lesley started to laugh.

'What's so funny?'

'You.'

'I'm glad you're amused.'

She held out her arms. 'Come here.'

He didn't move.

'I've made you angry.'

'No. I think I'll go. Let you rest before Veronica comes home.' He touched her face. 'I hate to see you like this.'

She stood up with him, small in her stockinged feet.

'It's raining.'

He looked at her raincoat on the chair. 'You weren't wet.'

'Dr Bader dropped me off. You've no coat.'

'I shan't get wet. It's a state of mind.'

She smiled. 'You're so good for me.'

'Like medicine.'

'I didn't mean that. I seem to be saying all the wrong things.'

He took her in his arms. 'As far as I'm concerned nothing you ever say or do is wrong. I love you completely.' He kissed her. 'You'll rest now?'

She nodded.

'I'll see you on Friday then.'

'Perhaps he's asleep?' Peach said hopefully to the Sister on the fourth floor. She wondered what he'd look like, whether there'd be bottles of blood above the bed, rubber tubing, evidence of things they were doing to him. The image of Parker, immobile, refused to form itself.

Sister smiled with her mouth her eyes thinking sheets and pillow cases and premed for number four and said no he wasn't asleep and she could go in last door on the right. There was a smell of lunch not long over laced with the disinfectant; outside each door a sinister trolley covered with a white shroud.

She raised her hand to knock on the door. A nurse came out of the room opposite and walked down the corridor with squeaky shoes.

There was no reply so she opened the wide door gently and went into the room. He was lying flat in the bed his legs beneath a cradle that made a pale mountain of the bedclothes.

'Didn't they tell you?' Parker said.

She stood horrified by the door. 'Only not to come.'

It was ten days now since they'd flown him back from France. I wouldn't go, Grant said, he's not really fit for visitors. Already there had been two operations on his face. He had nobody, Peach said, I have to go. She looked at his face. There were lacerations from nose to chin, chin to ear, crisscrossing the forehead, lumpily stitched.

She closed the door very slowly, skirted the bed and crossed to the window where there was a chair. She looked at the floor, the ceiling, the washstand with its thermometer in tidy little jar of disinfectant.

'Poor Baby,' Parker said.

'*I* should be consoling *you*.'

'I haven't looked in the mirror. Guess I don't need to now.'

She made herself look at the swollen nose, the slitty eyes. 'It's not as bad as that. It's just ... me.'

'I know you hate it.'

'Does it ... hurt very much?'

'There are moments. What does Henry say, Baby? About the leg.'

'I haven't seen Henry.'

'That's the sixty-four thousand dollar question. Everyone shuts up like a clam.'

There was a feeding cup beside the bed with a long spout.

'You don't fancy my chances either?'

'I told you. I haven't seen Henry. I don't know much about it.'

'You who have coreopsis for breakfast...'

'Coreopsis is a flower...'

'Don't change the subject. If I was a

doctor I'd reorganise everything in the interests of the patient. All right, Baby, come off the hook and tell me what it's like outside, if there is an outside, which I'm beginning to doubt.'

'Summer,' Peach said, relieved, 'English summer. Not hot. Roses everywhere. Rain. Everyone talking cricket.'

She realised what the room lacked; flowers. Could you bring flowers to a man? She could think of nothing more to say. Tried to convince herself that it was only Parker. He remained a stranger; ugly. The room waited quietly while she thought up and rejected topics of conversation.

'I might have killed you,' Parker said. 'I keep thinking of it.'

'You didn't.'

'It's the second time in my life I've been drunk. Really drunk. The other was when my Pop died.'

'I have to apologise,' Peach said.

'*You* have?'

'I was afraid to come back to the villa.'

'My God,' Parker said. '*You* did nothing.'

'I thought you were angry.'

'I pretended you were a Maggie. I knew perfectly well ... that all you cared about was that six-foot streak by the name of Henry. It happened to be convenience. I was sore all right; mad as hell; with myself.'

'It was me you went for in the car.'

'Like a mother when her kid runs in the road,' Parker said. 'She whacks it, bawls it out. It's herself she's bawling at for not looking after it better. Still wild about Harry?'

She nodded thinking Henry could look at the scarred face, lift the bedclothes...

'Funny after seeing him in the Diplomat ... they brought me here...'

'It's the best place for bone injuries.' She wanted to say tell me what he looks like, what he says.

'Tough about the car,' Parker said. 'I couldn't figure what had happened when I came to; guessed I'd made the Other Place and French was the language. You look good, Baby. I was hoping you'd come. When I get outa here we'll ... anything you like.' The effort was too much.

Peach stood up. Addressed the bed above his head. 'I'll come again.'

'Soon, Baby.'

'Soon. Bring you some flowers.'

He opened his hand on the bedclothes. She went without touching him.

There was roast chicken for dinner. Hilda carved with dexterity. Peach almost imagined a patient on the table.

Elliot had left in answer to an urgent call halfway through the soup. He came in now throwing a pillbox neatly onto the mantelpiece.

'Attempted suicide,' he said. 'I told the husband not to let her have the tablets.'

'Do you want your soup back?' Hilda said.

'No. I'll carry on. I'll have a wing if you can spare it.'

'Were you in time?'

'A lot of stuffing. Should be all right when they've washed her stomach out. Looking very glum, Peach. Thoughts of going back to College?'

'The conversation,' Grant said.

Elliot looked surprised. 'Have I said something?'

'I'm not going back,' Peach said. The image of stomach pumps had taken away her appetite for the chicken.

'What are your intentions, if one may ask?' Elliot said.

'She could always join the army,' Grant said.

'What on earth are you talking about?' The point of Hilda's carving knife neatly disarticulated the shoulder joint.

'Of shorthand typists,' Grant said. 'The salt of the earth. We could all retire.'

The decision had been sudden as she spoke. She knew she couldn't face another term trying to memorise Wade and Phillips, sitting through lectures in which she was entirely disinterested whose end product she didn't even care for. It was different for Sarah desperately keen to see herself in wig and gown.

'I went to see Parker,' she said.

Grant attacked his chicken. 'How did you find him?'

'You didn't warn me that he'd look so awful.'

'His face, you mean?' Grant said. 'That's nothing. Henry's coming to a decision about his leg tomorrow.'

'How do you mean?'

Grant had his mouth full.

Peach waited.

'Whether to amputate.'

She put down her knife and fork.

'Sorry. Didn't you know?'

'You aren't serious?'

'I'm afraid so. There's sepsis in the knee joint. He has to decide what to do.'

'That's absolutely terrible,' Peach said. 'Can you imagine...'

Grant pointed at her with his fork. 'Damned lucky he wasn't killed.'

She watched them eating, enjoying the chicken. It was like a play where the family sit calmly pretending to dine at one end of the stage while at the other some foul deed is being perpetrated about which the audience longs to shout, tell them, warn them. Dramatic irony. Hilda helped herself to gravy. Elliot chewed. They cared nothing for Parker, for the poor woman sick enough of life to try to leave it.

'Your dinner's getting cold,' Hilda said.

'I'm not terribly hungry,' Peace said. 'If you'll excuse me I'll go to my room.'

Two

The hospital, with its familiar smell absorbing sickness, death, with easy familiarity, puffed with its own importance, a miniature universe, floor quiet beneath the feet, doctors, administrators hurrying, visitors uncertain where to go; somewhere in the centre of the web was Henry.

Peach stopped a nurse in mid-flight.

'I'm looking for Mr Lindsay.'

'Letter.' She held out her hand.

'I'm not a patient. I just wanted to have a word with him if he has a moment.'

She looked up at the wall-clock. 'He's just finishing his outpatients. If you sit here you can go in when you see the last patient come out. The end door.'

She sat on one of the canvas chairs. There were several rows of them, dully brown, separated by a gangway. A deserted cinema except for the hideous pilgrimage down the side corridor of crutches, irons, wheelchairs, trolleys; a boy, his arm spread wide in an aeroplane sling, a fat girl with one leg. The nurse she had spoken to walked up and down the gangway with papers. A technician, holding wet X-rays carefully, went into Henry's room.

She waited ten minutes, twenty; it was foolish to have come; felt apprehensive as at the dentist's, reminded herself it was only Henry.

'You can go in now.'

The door of Henry's room opened slowly and a midget with an outsize medical boot he seemed scarcely able to drag limped out swaying heavily from side to side.

Henry had on a white coat and sat at a desk writing. There was a bed with a grey blanket, X-Rays on the screen, his jacket behind the door. He didn't look up.

'Sit down. Won't keep you a moment.'

The tone was reassuring. She imagined she was the midget, sick and afraid, and felt comforted. He finished the notes, neatly, meticulously. Put the card into a tray.

'Now!'

'It's me.'

He put down the pen.

'I've come about Parker.'

Henry picked up the pen again and held it between his two index fingers, carefully, as if it was important.

'Grant says you're going to amputate his leg.'

'Why are you so concerned?'

'It isn't funny to lose a leg, especially for Parker.'

'Why Parker especially?'

'He's keen on swimming, water-skiing...'
Henry was watching her. 'We had a row.
That's why Parker was drunk. I feel re-
sponsible.'

'You want the good fairy to wave her
magic wand and everyone to live happily
ever after.'

'Henry, please.'

He stood up and switched on the screen.
A plate with splintered-looking bones was
illuminated.

'This is Parker's leg,' he said deliberately,
pointing with his pen. 'The knee joint is full
of pus. We have treated the infection with
the usual antibiotics without success. The
next step is to amputate above the knee.' He
pointed at the plate with his pen.

She felt sick, wanted him to stop.

He switched off the screen and sat down at
his desk again, drawing neat boxes on his
blotter. 'As it happens I have decided not to
amputate. Not immediately that is. I had a
further swab taken from the pus this
morning and we have put it up against one
of the newest penicillins. Should the organ-
ism be sensitive...'

'When will you know?'

'We'll give it a few days, then it may be
possible to pin the bone fragments together,
so giving him at worst a stiffish leg.' He
shaded in the boxes he had drawn.'

'What are the chances?'

'Of success? I don't know. We shall have to be patient.'

'You don't care, do you?'

'In what way?'

'About Parker.'

'I'm not emotionally involved, if that's what you mean. Any more than I am with the achondroplasic dwarf who just went out. I'm sorry about Parker though and I'm doing everything I know. I'd do more if I could, especially since he seems to mean so much to you.'

He was making the wrong implications.

'How exactly did it happen?'

'We were on the Corniche at night. Parker had been drinking. We went over the edge.'

'You might have been killed.' He was angry. She didn't want him angry with Parker.

'It's history now Henry. I'm perfectly all right. Just Parker...'

He went back to the boxes.

The weight of the past lay between them. They had finished with Parker.

Henry stood up and started to take off his white coat.

'I'm keeping you,' Peach said.

'I start my list at two.'

He took his jacket from behind the door and replaced it with the coat, transferring his pen, tobacco.

'Thanks, anyway, for everything.' She stood up. Perhaps he would ask her for lunch. It was only just after one.

He buttoned his jacket. 'I'm sorry I can't promise more. Give Parker my regards.'

He went behind the desk again. There was nothing else.

'You know the way out?'

Peach nodded. 'I hope it works; the penicillin.'

'I hope so.'

Strangers.

She walked back through the empty Outpatients. In the main hall a man covered by a red blanket lay passive on a stretcher. A very pretty girl, smartly dressed, with a tanned skin and black hair, came in through the swing doors as Peach went out. She had clacked away on her high heels towards the Outpatients Department and Henry before it came to her with sudden clarity that it was the girl with the brown back.

Grant ran up the steps and along the corridor towards the Path. Lab and knocked on Lesley's door.

'Gone out love!'

He looked round. Two cleaners with scarves round their heads and green overalls were drinking tea in the scullery opposite.

'Any idea where?'

'Ask Boris Karloff there.'

One of them jerked a grimy forefinger towards the Lab where the chief technician

221

was bending over some slides.

'Do you happen to know where Dr Marshall is?'

The technician straightened up. 'Lunch. She went out about an hour ago with Dr Bader.' He looked at his watch. 'Should be back any time.'

'I'll wait.'

The man went back to his slides.

He went into Lesley's room and sat at her desk, swiveled from side to side in the chair, picked up the paper-knife, her pen, the framed photo of Graham, decided it was rotten being in love.

'It's like an appointment in Samarkand,' Peach said. 'The harder I run from hospitals the more I seem to become involved.'

She was at Sarah's, drinking Turkish coffee while Sarah filled the room with smoke.

'You should have come with me to Wales. Everything was green and beautiful; and father's Montezumas ... a sight for sore eyes.'

'You've put on weight.'

'Barnaby's cosseting. Like a mother hen; breakfast in bed, hot milk at night, ugh!'

'Did you tell her about the witch?'

'I didn't have to.' Sarah stirred her coffee and thought of Barnaby. She had got off the single decker bus which had brought her from the station and walked down the dusty road towards the little gate that led towards the old hen-house and through the garden. The rows of lettuces were browning at the edges. She pulled up a carrot, rubbed it clean and ate it. In the orchard the apples and pears were beginning to bend the branches. Barnaby was topping and tailing goose-berries at the kitchen table which was covered with faded oilcloth. I would love to take her to Heal's, Sarah thought, the kitchen department, eye-level ovens, Formica, spits, mixers, watch her face. There were copper pans on the Aga, polished brightly, the tiles were scrubbed white, bunches of onions and mint to dry hung from the ceiling, time refreshingly stood still.

'Barnaby.'

Panic. 'Miss Sarah ... fright of me life ... sitting here thinkin' on the dinner ... you should have said see ... carried your case from the bus did you ... cup of tea in a moment...'

Sarah kissed her. 'Why all the fuss, Barnaby?'

'The Judge told me you'd been ill. In trouble was you?'

'How do you know?'

She was fussing with the kettle. 'Bound to happen it was with all your shenaniging in London, no one looking after you. Always was a one for the boys see, never say no like your father.' She put the tea on the table and a whole fruitcake.

'I'm not hungry.' Sarah lit a cigarette.

Barnaby cut the cake and put a piece on Sarah's plate.

'Feed you up. Thin as a stick. And all that smokin's no good to you either.'

'What did you do?' Peach said.

'Lazed, fished, talked to father, did some climbing with him, my feet still haven't recovered.'

'Don't tell me there wasn't a man involved.'

'As a matter of fact there was.'

'I thought there must be. What's his name?'

'Miles.'

'Miles and miles and miles...' Peach poured more coffee.

'He's a barrister. He was appearing before Father. He brought him home for lunch.'

'What happened to Ronnie?'

'He got stuck in Rome with the girl in the white swimsuit. In addition to Miles I brought back a ham, a loaf of home-made bread and about a gallon of yoghurt. Barnaby insisted.'

'What's he like?'

'The antithesis of Ronnie. It's quite a change to see the bathroom tidy and know where everything is.'

The bell rang and Sarah disentangled herself from the coffee perquisites on the floor.

'In a moment,' she said, 'you'll be able to see for yourself.'

224

Three

She'd bought yellow roses. Already they were open, losing their colour.

'I'll bring more tomorrow.'

'How'm I doing, Baby?'

She adjusted the roses. 'You know you have to wait.'

'It's a reprieve, at any rate. I shall hang on to the leg for another few days. I've grown quite attached to it.'

'Grant says anyone else would have amputated. This penicillin you're getting is only weeks old.'

'Lucky for me the Prof. was in the States. The wonder boy is behind the ball all right. There's something about your Henry...'

'He belongs to the girl with the brown back.'

'Can't we give her a name?'

'Such as?'

Parker thought. 'Lulu.'

'Not enough class. Marcia.'

'Pollyana.'

'Dolores.'

'Virginia.'

He wasn't smiling, turned his head from side to side on the pillow.

'Are you in pain?'

'A little.'

He was sweating. She got up from the armchair.

He ran his tongue over his lips, which were swollen. The feeding-cup with its spout was next to the bed. She picked it up and held the spout to his lips, watching the beads of perspiration on his forehead.

'*Blanc de Blanc du Var,*' Parker said. 'Thanks, Baby.'

He was giving off heat like an oil stove.

'You're terribly hot.'

'She died of a fever and none could relieve her...'

She picked up a damp facecloth from the washbasin and sat down gently on the edge of the bed. She pushed back the hair, which was over his face and carefully mopped the patches between the scars.

'If there were more girls like you, less Maggies...' Parker said.

'You'd hate it.'

'I dreamed of a girl last night. I couldn't see her face but she had hair to her waist, a yellow dress. There was a hill and she held out her hand. I pulled her up to the top then we ran together down the other side, flying almost like two birds. When we reached bottom we collapsed together on the grass.'

'Must be a Maggie.'

'I dream a lot. Sometimes I'm swimming;

swimming farther and farther out to sea, I am infinitely strong, tireless … then I wake up, and all I can move is my arms, like a kitten.'

The sweat had broken out again on his face.

She swabbed tenderly at his forehead, over the swollen nose.

Parker watched her. 'Remember the first time.'

The day after she'd been to see Henry. The day she'd brought the roses. Parker had wanted a drink. She'd got up to call the nurse. The feeding-cup with the long spout was next to the bed. She'd picked it up, held it to his lips, her hand was shaking, the water trickled down his chin. After the first time it hadn't been so bad. She'd sat with him every day talking to him, watching the bruised face, touching him when it was necessary; willing him to get better; for Henry.

'I nearly drowned you.'

'You have improved. Given time you'd make a tolerable nurse. Seriously, Baby, you've made life bearable these last few days.'

'I want you to get better.'

He looked at her. 'Poor Baby. I know you do.'

'I'll sponge your arms.'

She pushed up the pyjama sleeves and sponged gently from elbows to fingertips, patting them dry with a towel.

'Better?'

'Much better.'

He was looking over her head.

She turned round. Henry, in dark suit, white shirt, stood at the end of the bed. The Sister in a frilled cap waited primly by his side.

'I didn't hear you come in.'

'You were busy.'

He looked at Parker. 'Not so good?'

'Not so bad. What are the chances?'

'Of saving your leg? Fifty-fifty.'

'Me and Peach are counting on you, aren't we, Baby?'

'I hope I don't let you down.'

The clock beside the bed ticked. Henry stood still looking at Parker. He's assessing the situation, Peach thought. General pallor, malar flush... I know him so well.

He took off his watch.

'Shall we have a look at the leg?'

'If you can call it that,' Parker said.

Peach stood up and put the facecloth back on the washbasin.

'I shan't be more than five minutes,' Henry said. The Sister helped him off with his jacket.

'I was going anyway.'

He rolled up his shirt sleeves and crossed to the washbasin, near enough to touch.

She said goodbye against the scrub of the nailbrush.

In the corridor she realised Henry thought she was in love with Parker.

Lesley dried the supper dishes and put them away haphazardly. Salt, pepper, two plates, the ladle...

'Mummy!'

'What do you want, Veronica?' The child stood in the doorway, her pyjama top unbuttoned.

'Something to eat.'

'Do yourself up and go to bed, there's a good girl.' She put a large plate beneath a pile of small ones in the cupboard.

'I'm hungry.'

'You can't be.' She hated drying saucepans.

'Look,' Veronica opened her mouth wide.

'You'll have to do your teeth again.'

'All right. What did you have for supper?'

'Spaghetti.'

'Ugh. Can I have a chocolate biscuit?'

'We haven't any. Only plain.'

'Salad, then.'

Lesley opened the little fridge and took a lettuce leaf from a polythene bag, giving it to Veronica.

'Salt?'

Lesley sighed and got the salt cellar out again.

'Don't be cross.'

'You know I don't like you to get out of

bed once you're settled.'

'But don't be cross.'

'I'm not cross.' She buttoned Veronica's jacket over the thin chest.

Veronica put the wet lettuce leaf on the back of her neck and kissed her.

'Good night, Mummy.'

'Good night. Straight to sleep.'

She put the salt away again and wiped the draining board, hating the wetness of the dishcloth. There were crumbs on the red lino, she kicked them with her foot, too lazy to sweep, then she took the broom and swept them into the dustpan.

The sitting-room was littered with Veronica's dolls, an old hat and a half-petticoat she used for dressing up. She switched on the radio, cricket scores, changed the programme, funny men, a crackle from the third, she switched off, picked up the blue-covered *Medical Journal*, 'Rickettsial and Viral Antibodies in Multiple Sclerosis … single specimens of sera were obtained from 36 patients…' the print blurred. It was almost nine. She wished she smoked, would welcome the business of a cigarette, removing it from the packet, lighting it, inhaling, exhaling the smoke, ridiculous really, people knew the dangers yet still continued, but then people were stupid, illogical… Two rings on the bell. She got up slowly, as if she was old, ill and opened the door.

'Thought you'd gone out,' Grant said.

'No.'

'What were you doing?' He came into the room.

'Nothing much. Reading.'

He picked up the *Journal*. 'Multiple Sclerosis. I suppose I shall have to start taking myself seriously, subscribing to all the journals. Do you realise this is my last day of freedom? Dogsbody Gatehouse, forty-eight hours on, forty-eight hours off. You'll have to come and see me when I'm on duty, I daren't slip out. If I did they'd be bound to bring in some messy street accident ... you're very quiet.'

'You're doing all the talking.'

'No, something's up.'

'Nothing.'

'Sure?'

'Sure.'

'Good. I've got news.'

'What is it?' She crossed the room and closed the window. She was wearing a dark green silk shirt; her red hair tangled with the collar.

'Come and sit down and I'll tell you. You're making me nervous.'

Lesley switched on the electric fire.

'It's sweltering,' Grant said.

'I'm cold.' She sat on the footstool and watched the bars become red.

'I am in a position to regularise our association,' Grant said.

'What do you mean?' She held out her hands to the fire, the fingers were slender, nails unvarnished, a gold wedding band on her left hand.

'We can get married.'

She turned to face him.

'I'll tell you what happened. I was getting pretty desperate about the situation, years of hospital jobs stretching ahead, never earning enough to look after you and Veronica, so I decided to discuss the whole thing with Dad. I thought he might have some bright ideas. As it happened he did. My grandfather, that's my mother's father, left some money, quite a bit, to Mother, for use in her lifetime, the remainder to go to Peach and myself on her decease. To cut a long story short they've agreed to give me an advance on the money to tide me over until I get a bit higher up the ladder.'

He watched Lesley's profile, she was looking again into the bright red bars of the fire.

'Don't you see, Les? It means we can get married!'

She said nothing and he moved to the floor beside her, taking her face in his hands and turning it to him. Her cheeks were warm beneath his fingers. He looked at the green eyes, grown so familiar, flecks of black, the soft lips.

'I love you, Lesley. You know that by now. If you don't love me as much, I understand. You haven't completely got over Graham. You will do. These things don't happen all at once. You'll come to love gradually, a little more every day. I worship you, you'll never know sadness or trouble again if I can help it; Veronica too, I may be a bit of a ham at first as a father but I'll do my best, I think she likes me...'

Lesley took his wrists and removed his hands from her face.

'Something *is* the matter?' Grant said.

'Yes.'

'You'd better tell me. I'll help you. Anything.'

'I'm sorry you've gone to all this trouble.'

'Trouble?'

'With your father.'

'It wasn't any trouble. He didn't mind. He wants to meet you. Properly, I mean.'

Lesley looked at him, one side of her face flushed from the fire, the other pale.

'I'm sorry Grant, I really am. I'm going to marry Nicholas Bader.'

Four

Grant woke abruptly and reached for his watch. Seven o'clock. He was due at the hospital at eight but had no desire to get up. No desire to do anything without Lesley. In films people shot themselves, took overdoses of drugs. Life was more difficult. You had to get through the slow torture of every day minute by minute. He'd been looking forward to starting the Casualty job; now he regarded the prospect, everything, with distaste. The day and the days to come stretched before him like an endless bog to be waded through; no joy, no Lesley.

'I'm going to marry Nicholas Bader.'

It wasn't a complete surprise, of course, that it was Nicholas Bader, whom he'd never met, and marriage. He'd known there was something on her mind, thought he could quiet it, smother it with love. What he'd thought, when he allowed himself, to be a doubt, a misgiving, he'd watched her struggle with it, had turned out to be love for someone else. There were no weapons, only resignation; no recriminations, only pain.

It was no less of a shock.

'I'm sorry Grant, I really am, I'm going to

marry Nicholas Bader.'

He looked at the watch. Time to go through the agony once more.

'I'm going to marry Nicholas Bader.' She looked into the fire, sat completely still, waiting for him to speak. He told himself it wasn't true, that he would always have Lesley. Everything he planned, wanted, included her. This other was an infatuation, a whim.

'How long has it been going on?'

'Since Graham died. Nicholas looked after him, you see. It's been an insidious thing, slow. I used him to lean on, there had to be someone, and he was always there. He never said anything, did anything, just his face, sometimes, when he thought I wasn't looking. I pretended I'd made a mistake, I hadn't seen. I didn't really want to know. He brought me home that day it rained. It might have gone on for years if it hadn't been for you.'

'Me?'

'You released a spring, brought to life what had lain dormant ever since Graham. I could smell the flowers, feel the sun, laugh, cry … when we came back from France everything was different. I couldn't be in the same room with Nicholas, within half a mile, it's hard to explain…'

'Not to me. I've been trying to get it across ever since I met. I know now why I never quite succeeded.'

'You'd be angry if I said I felt sorry for you. I despise myself too for what I've done to you. I can only say in mitigation that the last thing I wanted to do, ever, is to hurt you and that I know, I understand, exactly how you feel.'

The faint hum of the electric fire filled the room with sound.

Grant leaned forward but didn't touch her. 'Perhaps you'll get over it, Les?'

She looked at him, shaking her head, and it was the beginning of belief.

'How old is he?'

'Forty.'

'I see.'

'You see nothing.' She put her hands on his knees.

'Grant, if you knew how I felt about you, how I put off telling you...'

'It's cost you a little conscience but look how happy you're going to be!'

She took her hands away, flushed.

Grant went to the window, looked down at the bright lit windows of the launderette opposite.

'At least he'll be able to keep you and Veronica. You'll both do better out of than hanging around with me.'

'You know it's not that.'

'I wish I didn't. It's worse when you understand.' He walked round the room touching the sideboard, the radio, Veronica's doll. 'I can't visualise life without you, Les. Coming up here, being with you, talking to you, loving you.'

'I've tried to tell you.'

'I knew there was something. Just kidded myself it was imagination, anything.'

'Poor darling.'

'Please don't be kind. I never really stood a chance, did I?' Too young, stupid... I just filled a gap.'

'Grant.'

He looked at her.

'I want to tell you that you're the nicest person I've ever met.'

'What about Bader?'

'Nicholas is different. I love him.'

'I'd rather be loved.'

'We don't arrange these things.'

'Whoever does has a nasty little sense of humour.'

'You've done so much for me, for Veronica...'

'Please, Les. It's bad enough...'

'What will you do?'

'I'll have to get over it, won't I? Unless there's anything else you can suggest. I start my job tomorrow, don't forget.' He buttoned his jacket.

'Where are you going?'

'I'd better get an early night.'

She stood in front of him.

'Funny.' He indicated the room. 'It's like home. I can hardly believe this is the last time.'

'You'll come again.' It was without conviction.

'Goodbye, Les.' He held out his hand. 'I hope you'll be terribly happy and all that. You deserve it.'

She put her hand in his but he let it go and put his arms round her holding her close as if he'd break her body.

'Oh Les, say it isn't true. I've been dreaming.' He felt her tears on his neck. 'Don't cry. Just say something, anything.'

She said nothing. He savoured the feel of her body against his own for the last time, then released her. She sat on the arm of the chair drying her eyes.

He was surprised that he had the strength to get out of the door.

It was seven fifty-five when he pushed open the door of the Casualty Department; almost an hour and a half without her.

A skinny youth in a white coat and glasses was drinking tea.

'I'm Saunders. Just going off, hell of a night. You must be the new chap. That's Sister over there; put you in a picture. Must dash, whizzing down to an Auntie in Surrey. See you in forty-eight.'

Sister had black hair blue eyes.

'Top of the marnin' to you. We've a darlin' sebaceous cyst waitin' on you. Will I take your jacket for you, Doctor?'

Doctor. She was talking to him. What did one do with a sebaceous cyst? What other minor ops was he supposed to do? He looked at the door, wanted to bolt; he'd been so preoccupied with Lesley he'd had no time to be nervous. Alone in charge of the department for forty-eight hours. He prayed that nothing equivocal would come in. Perhaps conservative treatment for the cyst.

'Will I take your jacket for you Doctor?' A shade of asperity. Mustn't get on the wrong side of Sister, she was your ally, show you the ropes, stopped you making too much of an ass.

'This way then, Doctor, the trolley's laid up for you.'

'I still don't understand the technicalities of the thing,' Sarah said. She was painting the bathroom purple and standing on the edge of the bath to do the ceiling.

'Henry's giving him a new antibiotic,' Peach said. 'Hey, look out with that paint!'

'It can't drip, it's thyxotropic. Look!' She held the tin upside down.

'If it works he'll be able to pin the broken pieces together and save the leg. What are you looking at?'

'You. You wouldn't discuss a pimple on your nose.'

'I know. Something's happened. Since Henry's been looking after Parker I've been able to … do things, go near, touch him, you know what a mess his face is in; and I don't mind.'

'It's love, darling.' Sarah reached for the corner.

'But for the first time in years, in my life. You know how I feel, felt about these things. Funny, isn't it?'

Sarah brandished the brush. 'Not in the slightest. Girls have frozen stiff up to their whatsit's in water playing salmon, broken their nails on filthy old mountains, hiked their legs down to the knees, watched lunatics hurtling round Brands Hatch; all you have to do is listen to a few old bones now and again.'

'The odd part about it,' Peach said, while Sarah went back to the ceiling, 'is that Henry thinks I'm doing it for Parker.'

Sarah jumped down from the bath.

'You crazy loon!' she said.

'Why?'

'Because if you don't get down there and grab that man of yours the girl with the brown back will eat him alive and that will be the last you'll see of Henry.'

'I don't see what I can very well do under the circumstances,' Peach said.

'*Mama mia!*' Sarah put the can of paint and the brush in the bath. 'Go and put the kettle on darling and at the risk of having a patchy ceiling you and I will have to have a little talk.'

In the Casualty Department at Cat's, Grant handed the empty Horlicks cup to Sister. It had revived him a little.

'Sure and it's one of the busiest days we've had in along while,' she said, straightening her cap. 'I'll be going off now. See you in the morning Doctor and I hope you've a quiet night.'

'I hope so too, Sister. Good night and thank you.'

She'd been a tower of strength. He doubted if he could have got through the day without her. The clock on the wall said eight. Surely it couldn't be. He checked with his watch. He'd never known twelve hours go so quickly. He felt suddenly depressed and couldn't think why; remembered; Lesley. He hadn't had time to think. It all came back, flooding over him. Perhaps it was just as well he'd been working. Working. He'd never worked so hard in his life. There'd been the sebaceous cyst to start, a whacking great one on the neck of the Continental Booking Clerk from Thomas Cook's; then he'd sutured a head and a couple of fingers; examined a batch of admissions, organised X-Rays for a youth

241

who had come off his motorbike, looked like a fractured skull, didn't fancy the prognosis; incised an abscess; attempted to resuscitate a Dead on Admission in the ambulance; washed out a stomach, overdose of barbiturates, young girl jilted and 12 weeks pregnant, silly child, thought she'd be all right though, hoped so; first degree burn, boy of five playing with matches, couple of bee stings, cricket ball in the eye, nasty that one, that was about all except for the man in sudden cardiac arrest. External cardiac massage hadn't helped, half dead when they brought him in. Not bad for one day. Sister had been a brick. Telling him what to do without appearing to. Shall we open this one Doctor? Perhaps Mr Soames would like to have a peep at him, Doctor? Couldn't have managed without her. Hadn't let him lose face either in front of the patients. Half an hour's doze now if I'm lucky before supper.

He put a hand on his aching back to ease it, stuck his stethoscope in his pocket and walked out of Casualty into the main hall.

There were people everywhere, waiting, moving. He suddenly realised he was one of the staff. He walked towards the lifts, saw a flash of red hair, stopped in his tracks. She was moving briskly along the corridor leading to the wards. He dodged past a priest, a porter with a trolley. She had on a black suit, the light in the corridor was poor.

He pushed past a stout lady with a shopping bag.

'Who'd yer think yer shovin'?'

He took no notice. 'Lesley, Les!' He put a hand on her shoulder.

She turned round, a stranger, surprised.

'I'm terribly sorry.' He hadn't realised how tired he was. 'I thought you were someone else.'

Five

'Good afternoon.'

'Good afternoon,' Parker said.

'I'm Nurse Taylor and I'm going to get you ready for your op.'

'I love a lassie, a bonnie highland lassie!'

She bustled about the room tidying it. 'You'll no be feeling so bright when I've finished with you.' She picked up the newspapers from the bed and the floor, her apron crackling.

'You're new here, aren't you?'

'I'm up from Paediatrics.'

'It'll be a nice change for you then.'

'I don't know so much about that. You men are worse than babies.' She took the magazine he had put down.

'I hadn't finished reading that.'

'Look, you've to be ready in fifteen minutes or Sister'll be chasing me.'

'If I had the use of my legs I'd save her a job.'

'I'll tek care to kep out of your way in a week or two.'

'Humour the patient,' Parker said. 'Always allow him to think he's going to get better. You're a good girl, Maggie.'

'Taylor,' she said. 'Nurse Taylor.'

'I shall call you Maggie.'

'And I shall call Sister if I've any more nonsense.'

'Tell me about your boyfriend.'

'Who told you I have one?'

'Pretty girl like you.'

'If I have it's none of your business.'

'Please, Maggie!'

'His name's Stewart and he's a Pharmacy in Aberdeen, well it's his father's really but he's soon for retirement.'

'Aberdeen's a long way from here. What do you do on your night off?'

She was standing by the window filling a syringe.

'I curl ma hair. Will you roll your sleeve now for your pre-med?'

'Right or left?'

'It's all the same.' She squirted some of the fluid into the air.

'What's it for?'

'You've been twice to theatre and you know perfectly well. It'll make you nice and drowsy.'

'Will you stay and hold my hand?'

'Will you roll your sleeve or will I do it for you?'

'You can't. You'd get the syringe all un-sterile.'

'I'll count to three.'

'Don't trouble. I'll come quietly.'

Parker rolled up his sleeve. 'If I were Stewart I'd no be kickin' ma heels in Aberdeen. Ouch!'

Nurse Taylor put down the syringe, rolled down his sleeve and straightened the bed.

'There now. Try to have a wee sleep.'

'Will you be here when I wake up?'

'I daresay. For my sins.'

'Tell me about them.'

'They're no very sensational.' She picked up the kidney dish.

'Where are you going?'

'I'll be back. I've to wash number twelve. He's a real gentleman. Does as he's told. Are you feeling sleepy?'

'Just a "wee" bit. He's a lucky fellow.' Parker's speech was slurred.

'Who's that?'

'Yon laddie in Aberdeen.'

'Is there anything you want?'

Parker grinned.

'I'll be back in a while then.'

'On our own again' Elliot said.

'Grant's on duty,' Hilda said. 'He seems to be finding the work a bit of a strain.'

'It's not the work. It's the redhead. He thinks he'll never get over it.'

'She'll be far better off with Bader. She has the child to educate…'

'That's not the point. He worships her.'

'He'll get over it. They have some very

246

pretty nurses at Cat's.'

'I don't think you ever quite get over the first. You can put it behind you, improve on it even, but I think you ever completely recover. Mine was a girl called Clarice. She was the barmaid at the pub opposite Grey's where I did my midder, it's not there any more, I think it was a bomb. She had a waist so tiny I imagined I could circle it with my hands, I never got round to trying, and a beauty spot on her right cheek. I'd sit at the other side of the Public Bar spinning out my beer and wondering whether it was real.'

'Why didn't you ask her?'

'I never spoke to her. I didn't dare. I'd just sit there night after night with my beer watching her and working out how I was going to propose. I thought it would be the acme of happiness to live in a little room somewhere with that tiny waist and mass of piled-up black hair and the beauty spot. At that stage I remember exams intervened and there was no time for beer drinking. By the time they were over I had decided that the moment had come to approach her. I was going to put a foot up on a bar-stool, lean one elbow on the bar nonchalantly as I'd watch the other men do, and say "Hallo Clarice, what about a bite to eat one night?" Casually, as though I hadn't repeated it a hundred times to the mirror.'

Hilda smiled. 'And did you?'

'When I got back to the pub, I can't remember its name, something to do with horses, I think, she wasn't there. She'd gone off with a traveller from Wanstead, and there was a character called Bella behind the bar with whiskers on her chin. It was months I remember before I stopped dreaming about her. Even now, when I see a beauty spot, I automatically think Clarice. Grant won't get over this girl. Gradually he'll push the episode to the back of his mind but it will always be there, like Clarice. Peach I presume is at the hospital?'

'She goes every day. Whether she's trying to expiate her guilt because she feels a bit responsible for the accident I don't know. But for a girl who hates hospitals she's certainly spending a great deal of time there.'

'When I came in the other day,' Elliot said slowly, 'she was in the waiting-room with one of the builders from over the road. She was removing a foreign body from his eye.'

'Peach was?'

'Odd, isn't it? It could quietly easily have waited.'

'I wonder whether she's keen on Parker?'

'I presume we shall be informed when the time comes. Bright of Henry to save that leg of his.'

'He's a bright boy. I hope this pinning he's going to do will be successful.'

'Now that the infection has been overcome,' Elliot said, 'I'm sure he'll be all right.'

In the doctors' sitting-room there was a small coal fire in the grate. The chair cushions had been sat in and not shaken and the remains of the tray hadn't been cleared away.

'Grant said you wanted to see me,' Henry said. He closed the door behind him.

Peach was standing in the middle of the room.

'Yes I do want a word with you. How long is it going to take?'

'The op.? An hour or two. It's hard to say.'

He put his hands in his pockets, rocked back on his heels.

'It was lucky you tried him on that new drug.'

'Just one of those things,' Henry said. 'Fortunately the infection responded.'

Peach looked at the fire. It was Sarah's fault. She had told her to come. Now she could think of nothing to say.

'Silly really, a fire in September. I mean it isn't really cold.'

'It's the heating plant. Something wrong with it. I don't think it's working properly.'

'They never do.'

'How do you mean?'

'In hospitals. It's either too hot or freezing.'

'You've become quite an authority on hospitals.'

'Lately, yes. Sarah, Parker…'

'Poor Peach.'

'I don't mind.'

The sandy eyebrows went up. 'I thought you did.'

'Not any more. I can touch…'

'Parker?' He helped her. It hadn't been what she was going to say.

'Is the op. going to work? Will his leg be terribly stiff?'

'It's hard to tell at this stage. At least it will be his own.'

'Parker has tremendous faith in you.'

'He has courage. I like him.'

She felt the conversation thinning. Stupid of Sarah. Henry looked at his watch.

'What time are you starting?'

'They've taken him up to the theatre.'

'I'd better not keep you talking then.'

'Shouldn't be much more than an hour. You can sit here if you like. No one will mind. That's if you're going to wait.' He was halfway to the door.

She gathered her courage. 'Look Henry, I'll always wait. If you want me to.'

He stood still. 'If I want you to?'

'The girl; the one with the brown back.'

'You mean Diana.'

Diana the huntress.

'She's gone back to South Africa.'

'I thought…'

He waited, not making it easy.

'I put out my hand; to Parker.'

'I watched you.'

'There was a workman in the surgery. Everyone was out. I took some grit from his eye. He smelt terrible.' She looked at him.

'I did it for you.'

She sat in the armchair, exhausted. 'I can't make it any plainer.'

Henry went to the fire.

'These are moments,' he said. 'Parker, the workman's eye. There's a lifetime ahead.'

'I've had eighteen years. I know what it's going to be like.'

'You've hated them.'

'I didn't understand. I didn't want to understand. There was no love.'

He said nothing, leaning against the mantelpiece.

'I suppose Diana...' Peach said, getting up. She might as well go home.

He was watching her. 'There was never any danger.'

'Parker said...'

'Never mind what Parker said. There could never be anyone else.'

'You didn't want to see me any more. When I went to France you didn't write.'

'I wanted you to decide. It's a big decision.'

'I thought...'

'Don't think.'

That first night at the Lindsays'.

'Come here.'

She went to him.

'It'll be tibias for breakfast,' he said.

'Fibulas for dinner. I don't care.' She was in his arms and it was like coming home.

A porter in a green cap and gown opened the door.

'Theatre Sister sent me, Sir.'

'I'll be right up.'

'You'd better not change your mind,' Henry said. 'It'll be round the hospital in no time.'

'I was so afraid you'd changed yours.'

'You underestimate my love.'

'You didn't think I put out my hand … just for Parker?'

'Parker told me.'

'You knew all the time then. I should be angry.'

'Angry, anything; I love you.'

'They're waiting for you upstairs.'

'Then let me go.'

She sat in the armchair. 'I'd better start getting used to it.'

'I shan't be long.'

Peach smiled, the phrase echoing through her childhood.

He kissed the top of her head, her hand. 'You'll be here?'

'Of course.'

'Don't worry about Parker, darling; he'll be all right.'

Darling.
The door closed.
She was alone.
The fire settled in the grate.
She picked up a journal from a chair and opened it. 'A case of Pyrexia of very uncertain origin...'

This Large Print Book, for people
who cannot read normal print,
is published under the auspices of

THE ULVERSCROFT FOUNDATION

... we hope you have enjoyed this book.
Please think for a moment about those
who have worse eyesight than you
and are unable to even read or enjoy
Large Print without great difficulty.

You can help them by sending a
donation, large or small, to:

**The Ulverscroft Foundation,
1, The Green, Bradgate Road,
Anstey, Leicestershire, LE7 7FU,
England.**
or request a copy of our brochure for
more details.

The Foundation will use all donations
to assist those people who are visually
impaired and need special attention
with medical research, diagnosis
and treatment.

Thank you very much for your help.

THE FRATERNITY

It is the early sixties. The parents of law student, Peach Gatehouse, are both doctors and her brother is a medical student. She is in love with Henry but cannot contemplate life as a doctor's wife. Peach is attempting to make her own way in the world. Through her experiences and friendships she gradually learns to define her own needs and values and is confident about the decision she eventually makes about her future.

CHRISTIANITY

Christianity offers ... The question of the ... Jesus of Nazareth ... teacher ... Christians believe that Jesus ... the Son of ... Jesus ... death ... life after ... the world. Through his ... Christians seek ... believe, but also needs and values ... needs them. Jesus also taught his ...